'I have two presents for you,' Ross said. 'The first is just something that I thought you would enjoy... something to make you feel cosseted at the end of a hard day.'

He had bought her a silk robe, beautifully hand embroidered, and exquisite in its entirety. She gasped. 'It's lovely,' she murmured. 'I wasn't expecting anything—especially not this.'

'Hmm... I have to admit I've had a few problems over this robe—I keep thinking of how you would look when you're wearing it. I just can't keep up with the cold showers.'

Her cheeks flushed hotly pink, but he had already turned away, and now drew out a small box from the bureau. 'This is the present that I really wanted to give you,' he said softly. 'The trouble is, I'm not at all sure that you will accept it.'

The breath seemed to have left her body all at once. He opened up the box and inside, nestling on a velvet cushion, was the most perfect diamond ring she had ever seen.

Tears sprang to her eyes. 'Is that what I think it is?' she asked, her voice husky.

When **Joanna Neil** discovered Mills & Boon®, her lifelong addiction to reading crystallised into an exciting new career writing Medical™ Romance. Her characters are probably the outcome of her varied lifestyle, which includes working as a clerk, typist, nurse and infant teacher. She enjoys dressmaking and cooking at her Leicestershire home. Her family includes a husband, son and daughter, an exuberant yellow Labrador and two slightly crazed cockatiels. She currently works with a team of tutors at her local education centre, to provide creative writing workshops for people interested in exploring their own writing ambitions.

Recent titles by the same author:

HOT-SHOT DOC, CHRISTMAS BRIDE
THE REBEL AND THE BABY DOCTOR
THE SURGEON SHE'S BEEN WAITING FOR
CHILDREN'S DOCTOR, SOCIETY BRIDE

POSH DOC,
SOCIETY
WEDDING

BY
JOANNA NEIL

MILLS & BOON

First published in Great Britain 2009
Large Print edition 2010
Harlequin Mills & Boon Limited,
Eton House, 18-24 Paradise Road,
Richmond, Surrey TW9 1SR

© Joanna Neil 2009

ISBN: 978 0 263 21095 8

Harlequin Mills & Boon policy is to use papers that are
natural, renewable and recyclable products and made
from wood grown in sustainable forests. The logging and
manufacturing process conform to the legal environmental
regulations of the country of origin.

Printed and bound in Great Britain
by CPI Antony Rowe, Chippenham, Wiltshire

POSH DOC, SOCIETY WEDDING

CHAPTER ONE

THE doorbell made a cheerful jangle as Izzy walked into the village store, and the scent of freshly baked bread came to greet her, wafting on the air, teasing her nostrils and making her mouth water. Hunger pangs clutched at her stomach, causing her to frown momentarily. When had she last eaten? Could she count the couple of bites she'd taken from a sandwich several hours ago before all hell broke loose in A&E?

'You look as though you're ready to be off home, Izzy. Has it been a difficult day for you?' Mary the shopkeeper came forward from behind the counter, her all-seeing glance taking in Izzy's pale countenance, a smile softening her features.

'You could say that.' Izzy's mouth made a faint curve in response. Mary was a motherly figure, always ready to talk, the sparkle in her blue eyes belying the years hinted at in her grey hair. 'Unfortunately there was a triple-car accident on the dual carriageway earlier, and we were kept busy for most of the day dealing with all the casualties. We patched up the ones who were really badly injured, and sent them on to the hospital in Inverness.' Izzy broke off to glance around the shop, taking in the wide assortment of goods on display.

Mary nodded. 'I heard about it on the local radio. I guessed they would be taken to your A&E first of all, it being the nearest. It was a marvellous day when they gave the go-ahead to set up the unit next to the health centre, wasn't it? You and your doctor colleagues must have helped so many people there over the last few months.'

'It's true we've been in demand.' Izzy turned her gaze from shelves filled with household essentials and pushed back a swathe of chestnut coloured hair that had fallen across her cheek. 'Living here in the Highlands, people have always faced a long journey to hospital, but now the new A&E unit acts as a halfway station. Knowing it had been given the go ahead was one of the things that drew me back here…that and the fact that I can go out as an immediate care responder. It makes for variety and gives me a sense that I'm doing something worthwhile.'

Izzy's gaze wandered again. She had dropped in here planning to pick up a set of teacloths for her kitchen, but her senses were filled with the appetising aroma of hot meat pasties and oven-fresh bread.

Mary smiled. 'I guessed you would come back to us before too long…once you had completed your medical training. This place is in your blood. You were always one to love the hills and the mountains, and I remember when you were a teenager you could often be found down by the harbour, watching the boats.'

The shopkeeper contemplated that for a moment or two, but then her face straightened, her mouth pulling in a flat line. 'Unlike some I could mention. You'd think the Laird would put in an appearance at the castle from time to time, wouldn't you, instead of leaving everything for Jake Ferguson to handle? Not that Jake's done a great deal to help things along in the Laird's absence... And now it looks as though he'll be doing even less, if it's true he's thinking of moving down south to be with his daughter.'

'Is he?' Izzy raised a brow. No wonder she hadn't received a reply to her request for various repairs to be carried out on her rented property. Jake obviously had other things on his mind. Why was she the last to know what was going on in the village? Her mouth made a rueful quirk. That was what came of working all hours and trying to mind her own business.

'That's what Finn the postman reckons.' Mary was frowning. 'He's always the first to know the gossip.' She gave a small gesture of dissatisfaction at the complexities of life before gathering herself together once more. 'Anyway, what can I get for you today, Izzy?' she asked. 'Will you be wanting a loaf of bread to take home? I've just brought a batch fresh from the oven, and I know how much you like it.'

'Thanks, Mary. That would be lovely…and a couple of those pasties, too, since I'm in no mood for cooking today. I'm so hungry I could eat one here and now.'

'Then you must do that,' Mary said with a chuckle, handing her a pasty along with a serviette.

'Thanks. You're a life-saver.' Izzy took a bite, savouring the tender meat and flaky pastry before brushing crumbs from her mouth. 'Mmm…that's delicious.' She closed her eyes fleetingly, to better relish the experience. 'And will you add a bag of my father's favourite mint sweets? I'll drop them off to him on my way home. And my mother's magazine, if it's come in.'

'Aye. I can do all that. And we've a new batch of diaries in, ready for the New Year, if you're interested. I'm very taken with them, with the gold embossed lettering and the soft feel of the leather.'

Izzy glanced over to the display rack where the diaries were set out, and paused to run a clean index finger lightly over the cover of one that stood to the front. 'You're right—and I will take one with me, before they're all snapped up.

They're beautiful, aren't they?' She gave a gentle sigh. 'If only we could really start afresh with each year that comes along. We've still a few weeks to go before then, though, haven't we? It seems like an eternity. These last few months have been so difficult, in one way or another... For all of us, not just for my family. I can't say I'll be sorry to see an end to this year.'

'Me, too.' Mary put in a heartfelt acknowledgement. 'The business is limping along, but I'm not alone in that...all the villagers are having a tough time of it.'

Izzy nodded, taking a moment to finish off her pasty before wandering over to the shelves where the teacloths were stacked. 'The crofters haven't been doing too well, have they?' She frowned, pausing to pick up a linen cloth, holding it up to the light of the window. It was pleasingly decorated with a Highland scene, depicting a shimmering loch bordered on either side by craggy, heather-clad mountains. 'I know the harvest was poor this year, so it's probably just as well the majority have other jobs to keep them going.'

'It is,' Mary acknowledged, 'but I can't help thinking you've come off worse than any of us, with your cousin Alice being in hospital and all. Your poor mother was terribly shaken up by it, I know.'

'Yes, it hit us hard, all of us—my mother especially. Hearing about the car crash came as a dreadful blow. After all, Alice lived with us for a few years after her parents passed away, and she was more like a sister to me.' Izzy was still shocked by the thought of the accident that had kept Alice in hospital these several months. It saddened her that she was helpless to do anything to speed up her recovery, and it wrung her heart that there was so much bitterness and recrimination associated with the whole event.

Her father had never reconciled himself to the circumstances that had taken Alice away from them, some six or seven years ago, and now her return to Scotland was tinged with unhappiness.

She tried not to think about it. Instead she looked out of the window at the landscape of her birth, a sight that invariably had the power to calm her. In the distance she could see the glorious hills and mountains of the West Highlands, with white painted houses clustered along the road that wound gently through the glen, and if she looked very carefully she could just make out the curve of the bay and the small harbour where boats bobbed gently on the water.

Bringing her glance closer to home, she looked to where the side road led on to the paved fore-court of the village shop. She thought she heard the soft purr of an engine drawing closer. Moments later a gleaming four-by-four made an appearance, gliding to a halt in front of the store.

'Well, there's a vehicle that makes a grand statement, if ever there was one.' Mary came to join her by the window, and both women looked out at the majestic silver Range Rover that had come into view. 'Now, who do you think that belongs to?' the shopkeeper queried absently. 'No one from around here, that's for sure.'

Izzy didn't answer, but watched as the driver slid down from the car and walked purposefully round to the passenger side. He pulled open the door and reached inside the vehicle, resting his arm on one of the seats as he paused to speak to someone who was sitting in the back.

Perhaps it was the casual, loose-limbed confidence in the way he moved that caught Izzy's attention, or maybe it was the taut stretch of black denim straining against his strong thighs that alerted her, or even the sweep of his broad shoulders, clad in a supple leather jacket... Either way, Izzy's senses were suddenly geared into action. A band of tension tautened her abdomen. She realised there was something intensely familiar about the rugged, long-legged man who had come out of the blue to fill her vision.

Right now he was inviting a tawny-haired child to step down from the vehicle, and when the girl hesitated he lifted his arms to grasp her with both hands and swing her effortlessly from her seat, setting her carefully down on the ground. For a second or two, as he paused to steady her, he looked towards the far hills, so that his features came momentarily into sharp relief. Izzy pulled in a brief, harsh breath of recognition.

What had Mary said about the Laird not coming home? She watched as he stood aside to encourage a young boy to jump down from the car, and beside her Mary echoed what they were both thinking.

'Well, I never. Talk of the devil. If it isn't himself, come to grace us with his presence. And aren't those children with him your Alice's bairns? I thought they were staying with their aunt, Alice's sister, down in the Lake District?' She frowned. 'I wonder what brings him to these parts after all this time? How long has it been? About six years, do you think?'

'That sounds about right.' Izzy struggled to find her voice. 'It must be all of six years since the old Laird died.'

'And hardly a sight of the new Laird since— though I suppose he must have been in touch with his estate manager on a fairly regular basis. How else would Jake have had the power to put the rents up and cut the timber hereabouts? Things could be falling apart up at the castle, for all Ross Buchanan knows. That's what comes of being an absentee landlord. Everything goes to rack and ruin.'

Izzy was still struggling to come to terms with seeing Ross back on his home ground, but now she stifled a discomfited laugh. 'You're beginning to sound an awful lot like my father,' she murmured.

Mary chuckled. 'And your father doesn't even have the excuse of being a tenant, does he? Now, there's a man with more than his fair share of common sense.'

'I think it has rather more to do with a determination never to be indebted to the Buchanans in any way,' Izzy said with a rueful smile. 'He's a fiercely proud man, my father.'

The sound of children's excited voices floated on the air, coming closer, and Izzy felt her whole body tighten as she waited for the shop door to open. How was she going to cope with coming face to face with Ross Buchanan after all this time?

'I'm thirsty,' the boy said, bursting into the store with the noisy rush of energy of a youngster who had been imprisoned inside a car for far too long. At six years old, he had no time to waste. Life was for living. 'Can I have a can of fizzy pop?' He directed the words behind him as he continued on his path. 'I'm not going to be sick again. You said I could have a drink, and I really want fizzy pop…and an ice cream with lots of sprinkles on it and a chocolate flake.' He headed towards the snacks section.

The girl followed him in a slower, more measured fashion, taking time to look around. The lingering rays of afternoon sunshine lent glimmering highlights to her hair, and Izzy saw that her green eyes were thoughtful, as though she wanted to weigh up the situation before making any decisions. She was younger than the boy, about five years old, and a pretty girl, so much like her mother, but with a shy expression. Now she put out a tentative hand to examine a packet of potato chips, only to have the item whipped out of her fingers by her brother.

'I saw it first,' he said. 'They're barbecue flavour and that's my favourite and it's the only one.'

'You snatched it from me,' the girl protested. 'Give it back.'

'You'll stop fighting this minute, both of you,' Ross said in a quiet, authoritative voice, 'or neither of you will have anything. You're on someone else's property and you will respect that.' He held out a hand for the crisp packet.

The boy's mouth clamped in a mutinous line, and he glared at his sister. She sent him back a daggers-drawn look, sparks of steel arrowing towards him, her body poised ready for action.

Ross retrieved the offending packet and glanced at Mary, who had stepped forward. 'I'm sorry about that,' he said softly, his voice a low rumble like smooth velvet trailing over a roughened surface. 'They're usually much more well behaved, but they've been cooped up in the car for a few hours. That was my fault—I wanted to get here before nightfall.'

'That's all right,' Mary answered. 'Perhaps they might like to run around out back for a while and let off a bit of steam? There's a patch of grass and some wooden benches where they could sit and eat, and there are some swings. We don't have the café operating now, since the tourist season has finished, but the facilities are available for them to use, and they can take a snack out there with them if you like.' She looked fondly at the children, who were optimistically replacing glowers with cautious, expectant glances.

'Thanks, Mary. I appreciate that. I'm sure that will be just the thing.' He studied her, a brief, all-encompassing look that took in her neat skirt and blouse and the softly styled hair that framed her face. 'It's good to see you again. You're looking well.'

'Thank you. And the same goes for you… Though we were just saying that we were surprised to see you back here after all this time. But perhaps you're here to see Alice, now that she's been brought up to Inverness?'

'We?' Ross glanced around, but Izzy had already moved forward, pausing to crouch down and say hello to the children.

'Molly, Cameron—it's so lovely to see you again.' She hugged them both, and they in turn smiled a bright-eyed welcome.

'Auntie Izzy, you came to my birthday party,

do you remember?' Molly's eyes were shining with happiness. 'You bought me a dolly, and you and Mummy baked cakes for tea. And then the next day we went down to the lake for a picnic.'

'I remember it well,' Izzy said. 'We had such a lot of fun, didn't we?'

Molly nodded, her expression gleeful.

'Mum's in hospital now,' Cameron said, his gaze solemn. His hair was dark, like his father's, and his eyes were grey. 'She hurt her head and her leg and her arm, and she can't walk very well. We're going to see her tomorrow.'

'I know, sweetheart. Your mother's been very poorly, hasn't she?'

He nodded. 'We've been to see her a lot in hospital where we live, but now they've moved her.'

'But it's all right,' Molly put in, 'because she needs to learn to walk about and do things, and they have a place at the new hospital where they can help her.'

'That's good, isn't it? I'm sure the doctors will look after her very well.' Izzy stood up and waited as Mary shepherded the children towards the garden area at the back of the shop.

'Your uncle says you can have these buns to eat, and you're to share the crisps,' Mary told them as they eagerly walked with her. 'I'll bring the drinks, and maybe you can have ice creams a little later, once you're settled.'

She left the shop, and Izzy realised the moment could not be put off any longer. She straightened her shoulders and forced herself to take a good look at the man who had played havoc with her feelings over a good stretch of time. Tall, striking in appearance, with black hair dark as midnight, he was the devil incarnate, sent to try her with his powerful presence and his innate authority descending over everyone and everything.

She looked into Ross's eyes and found herself trapped, submerged in those blue-grey depths, only to falter as she had always done when he was anywhere around.

'We had no idea that you were planning on coming here,' she murmured. 'It's been such a long time since your father's funeral that we felt sure you had decided to stay away for good.'

'And now my coming back here will well and truly set the cat among the pigeons, I dare say.' There was a glint in his eye that told how he relished that thought. 'I know there are those who would much prefer never to set eyes on me again, but sadly they're in for a disappointment. Your father will most likely be sharpening his axe at the first whisper of my return... The battle between the Buchanans and the McKinnons is set to run and run, isn't it?'

She wasn't going to let him get away with that. 'From what I've seen, you seem to thrive on any skirmishes that come your way. You've never been one to back down from a fight, have you?' Her chin lifted. 'That's why you and your own father were at loggerheads the whole time. Two stubborn men coming face to face will always clash, and it's the same with you and my father. Neither one of you will ever consider taking a different course. That would be too simple, wouldn't it? It would reek too much of losing face.'

He raised a dark brow. 'Why should I want to change my ways? I've done nothing wrong— and, more to the point, I'm the only one left to uphold the Buchanan name.' He stood before her, his long legs taut, his back ramrod-straight, as though daring her to deny it. 'That might not seem important to you, but it's something that lays heavily on me.'

'Of course it does,' she retorted, her grey eyes smoky with mocking amusement. 'That's why you left it to Jake to do what was necessary. Do you think any of us here care a jot about the Buchanan name? Whether the landlord is a Buchanan or not, he's still going to look after himself first.'

He laughed. 'You haven't lost any of your straight-talking ways, have you, Izzy? That's what I always liked about you. You could be relied on to put me right if I looked to be veering off course.' He reached out to gently cup her face in his palm. 'As I often did. But then I was young and foolhardy, and reckless was my middle name.' His voice softened to a whisper. 'It's good to see you again, sweet Isabel McKinnon.'

Izzy's skin heated where his hand lightly trailed over her cheek. The lightest touch of his fingers was enough to fire her blood, and she didn't know why he had the power to do this to her—to make her senses quicken and her heart pump faster.

It was frustrating, and above all it wasn't fair, this hold he had over her. He was the enemy, he was everything she should rebel against, and yet… And yet her body ignored every warning, flouted common sense and instead abandoned her to the powerful onslaught of his devil-may-care charm whenever he came near.

It wasn't to be borne, and out of desperation she decided that attack was the best form of defence. 'You might not be so pleased once you settle in at the castle and see how many complaints I've lodged with your estate manager. Or perhaps you aren't planning on staying around all that long?'

'Long enough to take the scowl from your mouth, perhaps,' he said, tucking his hand under her jaw and swooping to drop a fleeting, fierce kiss on her soft lips.

She gasped as the imprint of his mouth registered on her, leaving a tingling explosion of sensation in its wake. Her whole body responded in a surge of fizzing excitement. 'You…you kissed me,' she said in shocked wonder.

Heat shimmered in his gaze, laughter dancing in the blue-grey depths of his eyes. 'I couldn't resist,' he said, letting his hand fall from her. 'But I was right, wasn't I? It certainly lifted the scowl from your lips, and it only took… what…all of two seconds?'

She waited a moment or two while she battled to bring her emotions under control once more. 'I wonder if you should have more pressing things to do with your time?' she said finally, for want of any more cutting response. 'I think the children may well need your attention. Or perhaps you'd forgotten all about them?'

'I would never do that. But far be it from me to give you cause to find me wanting,' he murmured. 'I'll go right away and find out what they're up to.' He paused, though, to study her slender figure, letting his glance sweep over her from head to toe, taking in the clinging cut of her jeans and the soft cashmere of her top. 'Still as beautiful as ever, my lovely Izzy. But a sight more feisty than when last we met, I dare say, and with way more delicious curves.' His mouth curved. 'Yum.'

Her grey gaze narrowed on him. 'You should watch your step, Buchanan,' she said in a low, controlled tone. 'You're not so big you can't take a tumble.'

He put up his hands in self-defence. 'Okay, okay. You can stand down. I'm an unarmed man.' He made a mock attempt at wiping his brow with the back of his hand as she finally relaxed her shoulders. 'Phew! And I thought young Molly could shoot sparks. They're nothing compared with her aunt's artillery.'

He was chuckling as he moved away in the direction of the garden, and Izzy stared at him, firing more darts at his straight back. The man was dangerous—a hazard to all unsuspecting women who suffered under the misapprehension that he was a good-natured, easy-going kind of man. He could effortlessly take your heart and squeeze it dry.

But that was probably the least of her problems right now. How on earth was she going to break the news to her father that Ross Buchanan was back in town?

CHAPTER TWO

'WOULD you like more coffee? I just made a fresh pot.' Izzy's housemate lifted the coffee percolator, letting it hover over two brightly painted ceramic mugs in the centre of the kitchen table.

'Yes, please… Anything to warm me up. It's freezing in here.' Izzy chafed her arms with her hands in an effort to drum up some heat. 'We really need to get that central heating fixed, or at the least buy a portable heater.' She frowned, gazing around the room. 'I suppose I could make some toast—the heat from the grill will probably make us feel better.'

Lorna nodded. 'Good idea. I'll fry some bacon. I'm really in the mood for toasted bacon sand-wiches to set me up for a day in A&E.' She grinned. 'Just in case we don't make it down to the cafeteria again.'

'Good idea.' Izzy took out a loaf of bread from the wooden bin. 'But I've been thinking… We could take our own food in to the hospital—sandwiches, biscuits, cereal bars…anything that we can cover with clingfilm and set out on a trolley. That way we'll have stuff on hand if things get hectic.' She smiled. 'I thought it was great when Greg brought in hot sausage rolls and pastries the other day. They gave me the will to go on.'

'Me, too.' Lorna replaced the coffeepot on its base and went to get a frying pan from the cupboard. 'As to the central heating, and all the other repairs that need doing around here, I suppose Ross will need a bit of time to settle in before he gets round to sorting things out. That's if he means to stay, of course. It could just be that he's brought the children over to be closer to Alice, and once she's up and about he'll be off.' Lorna hesitated, frying pan in hand, thinking things through.

She was a slender girl, with a mop of fair hair

that had a flyaway look about it, as though it was permanently out of control—pretty much on a par with her bubbly character. Just now, though, her blue eyes were thoughtful. 'Then again,' she murmured, 'he always had a bit of a thing for Alice, didn't he? In fact, if you recall, the rumour was that she was seeing Ross long before she decided to run off with his brother. Quite the scandal at the time, I hear.'

'Yes, it was.' Izzy frowned. 'Especially where my father was concerned. He hated the thought that she had anything at all to do with any of the Buchanans.'

Lorna placed the frying pan on the hob and turned towards Izzy, throwing her an anxious look. 'Oh, I'm sorry, Izzy…I was forgetting for a minute that she's your cousin. I didn't mean to say anything out of line—it's just that everyone's talking about Ross coming back here. People are wondering what's going to happen about the crofts, and whether they can do anything to improve the general standard of living. And on top of all that they're buzzing with talk about the way your families have been at each other's throats for as far back as anyone can remember. There doesn't seem to be any getting away from it. Of course they're all siding with you and your parents and Alice.'

'It's all right, Lorna. I knew as soon as I saw Ross was back in Glenmuir that the tongues would start wagging. I don't know *what* he's going to do about the crofts. Most people hereabouts lease the land and the cottages from him, but I imagine he'll have to put his own house in order before he can find time to look into any concerns they might have about their livelihoods. I suppose he could always say that what they do with the land is up to them for the term of the lease.'

'Not his problem, you mean?' Lorna pulled a face. 'You could be right. But people seem to think Ross should do something so that they can make a decent living from the land. It's history rearing its head once again—you know how it is…people around here don't let go of the past easily. They're convinced their rights were taken from them in the Highland Clearances well over a hundred years ago. At the very least they think he should pay them compensation on behalf of his ancestors.'

Izzy switched on the grill and set bread out on the rack. 'That's fighting talk,' she said with a husky laugh. 'But, knowing how the Buchanans operate, I doubt it will get them very far. They've always known how to manoeuvre their way through the legal system and come out the winners.'

'I'm told the Buchanans have oodles of charisma when they choose to exert it, and none of it lost on the women who cross their paths…' Lorna turned the heat on under the pan and added rashers of bacon. 'That was the start of things with your families, wasn't it?' she asked. 'Your father's great-aunt being seduced by the former Laird—Ross's great-grandfather—some eighty odd years ago.'

'That's very true.' Izzy slotted the grill pan under the heat. 'Of course it caused all kinds of anger and heartache and general mayhem when she died in childbirth. That really upset the

McKinnons and added fuel to the fire. I think my father, when he was growing up, soaked up all the vitriol that was poured on the Buchanans, and consequently he has no time for them.

'Alice going off with Robert Buchanan was history repeating itself, and that well and truly stirred the melting pot, didn't it?'

'What happened when Robert and Alice took off?'

'My father exploded, but at least he directed most of his anger towards Robert back then. I suppose it made things worse because Alice had been seeing Ross to begin with, and at least he was the steady one, whereas Robert always had a wild streak.'

Alice and Ross… Izzy shied away from that thought. How deep had their feelings been for one another before Alice had turned to Robert? Did Ross still care for her in the same way? She pulled herself together, aware that Lorna was waiting for her to go on.

'Alice was young, and had obviously been led astray by both Buchanans,' she said, 'but for all that my father wouldn't forgive her. He's never had much to do with her children, either. My mother has always kept in touch with the family, by letter and the occasional visit, but she's very wary of what my father would have to say on the subject. She keeps things low-key and tries not to provoke him.'

She frowned. 'The only real difference, for all the scandal that it caused, was that Robert Buchanan was never going to be the new young Laird.' Izzy pondered the situation as she laid hot toast down on the plates. 'I can't help wondering if that was what lay behind all the resentment simmering between him and Ross. As the older brother, Ross was the one to take over the estate. Robert always wanted what Ross had, and unfortunately that included his girlfriends.'

'That must have been some sibling rivalry.' Lorna added tomatoes to the pan, and it wasn't long before the appetising aroma of sizzling bacon filled the air.

The kitchen was much warmer now, and Izzy began to place the plates on the table, ready for the meal. She was setting out cutlery when there was a loud knocking on the door.

'I wonder who that can be,' she said with a frown. 'It's barely seven-thirty in the morning. Who else would be up and about at this time of the day apart from farmers, doctors and the milkman?'

'I did notice the milkman giving you the eye the other day,' Lorna remarked with a hint of mischief. 'I thought at the time he was just surprised to see you open the door at that hour, but I may have been wrong about that.'

Acknowledging that with a smile, Izzy shook her head. 'You have such a lively imagination.' She went to find out who was there.

A moment later she stared down at the two children who were standing on the doorstep, her brows lifting in astonishment. 'Molly, Cameron—I wasn't expecting to see you.' She glanced around to see if anyone had come with them, but nothing stirred on the path that led down the hill except for a solitary bird that took flight from the nearby copse. 'Have you come here all by yourselves?'

'Yes,' Molly said. 'It isn't far to here from the castle, and we remembered where you lived from last time we came to visit.' She frowned. 'Uncle Ross wasn't staying with us then, though.'

'No, we came here with Mum,' Cameron put in. 'Dad stayed at home.' A momentary sadness washed over his thin face. 'He's not here any more, you know,' he said earnestly. 'Mum says he was hurt in the car accident and they couldn't make him better, but he's peaceful now.'

'I know, sweetheart.' Izzy wanted to put her arms around the children and make everything right again, but it was an impossible task. How could she begin to comfort them for the loss of their father? She contented herself instead with making them welcome, putting an arm around their shoulders and ushering them into the house. 'Come into the kitchen. It's warmer in there.'

'Mummy's not going to go away, as well, is she?' Molly asked, her voice hesitant. 'She was in the car with Daddy, and she was hurt.'

'No, Molly. Your mother is getting better every day. It will take some time before she's on her feet properly, but before too long she should be back with you.'

'In the New Year?' Cameron suggested. 'That's what Uncle Ross says…some time in the New Year.'

'That sounds about right to me,' Izzy said. Her cousin would recover well enough from the broken bones she had sustained in the car crash, but she had also suffered head injuries and internal bleeding that added substantially to her problems. The head injuries meant that she had no memory of the accident itself, though thankfully her faculties had been spared. It was hoped that in time she would make a full recovery.

She pushed open the door to the kitchen and showed them inside.

Cameron sniffed the air appreciatively. 'Are you making breakfast?' he asked in a hopeful tone, his eyes widening.

'Yes, we are.' Izzy nodded. 'Looks like we have more people to share the sandwiches,' she told Lorna. 'Do you think we can run to a couple more?'

'I think we can manage that. I'll add a bit more bacon to the pan.' Lorna smiled at the children, and then, as they stared about the room, taking everything in, she surreptitiously lifted questioning brows towards Izzy at their arrival so early in the morning.

Izzy hunched her shoulders in a bemused gesture before turning her attention back to the children. 'Sit yourselves down by the table,' she said. 'So, your Uncle Ross knows you're here, does he? Hasn't he given you anything to eat?'

'He's asleep,' Molly said, shaking her head so that her curls quivered. 'I tried to wake him, but he didn't even open his eyes… Well, just the corner of one, a tiny bit. Then he closed it again and made a sort of "hmmph" from under the duvet, and buried his head in the pillow.' She lifted her arms to show the extent of her helplessness.

Izzy's mind conjured up an image of Ross, his dark hair tousled from sleep, his limbs tangled in the folds of the duvet. It made her hot and bothered, and she quickly tried to banish the errant thought from her head.

'And I'm starving,' Cameron confirmed. 'I couldn't find the breakfast cereals in any of the cupboards, so I went to look for Maggie, but she wasn't anywhere around.'

'I imagine it's a bit too early for the house-keeper,' Lorna commented. 'From what I've heard she doesn't usually go up to the castle until after nine o'clock.'

'Well, we didn't know what to do, so we decided to come and see you,' Molly finished trium-phantly. 'I remembered that you live at the bottom of the hill…and that you always have a cookie jar on the worktop. I remember it's a yellow bear with a smiley face and a Tam o' Shanter hat.'

'That's right.' Izzy pointed to the corner of the room, where the ceramic cookie jar sat next to the microwave oven. 'There he is, just as you said. Perhaps you could have a cookie after you've eaten your sandwich?'

Pleased, Molly nodded, while Cameron fidgeted in his seat and asked pertinently, 'And me, too?'

'Of course. I wouldn't dream of leaving you out, Cameron.'

He looked suitably appeased at that, and Izzy concentrated on making them both a sandwich. Pushing the plates towards them, she looked from one to the other. 'So your uncle doesn't have any idea that you've come here?'

Cameron shook his head, looking uncertain, but Molly, after taking a bite from her sandwich, said, 'I left a note for him on the kitchen table to let him know we'd come here. Mummy said we should always make sure someone knows where we are.'

'Mmm, that's good. That was the sensible thing to do,' Izzy said with a smile. 'I think I'd better give him a ring all the same, as soon as we've eaten, just to make sure he knows what's going on, or he might be worried.' She wasn't going to let her sandwich go cold on his account, though. That was supposing he was even awake by now, of course. But if he wasn't she would simply let the phone ring until he answered it. How could the man be so careless as to let the children run loose at such a young age? 'Lorna and I have to go to work soon, you see, otherwise you would be able to stay here. Perhaps we'll take you back home when we've all eaten.'

'That's okay,' Cameron said. 'I said you'd probably have to go to the hospital. I remembered from last time we were here.'

Izzy sat down to eat her toasted sandwich with Lorna and the children, chatting to them about life up at the castle. 'Are you settling in all right?' she asked.

Molly nodded. 'It's kind of exciting. There's loads of rooms and we can go in any of them.'

'And there's a winding staircase that goes up and up,' Cameron said. 'And there are lots of doors. I nearly got lost, and Uncle Ross had to come and find me. He said I was in the pantry, but it was big—like a room.'

A few minutes later Izzy left them talking to Lorna while she went into the hall to phone Ross in private. It was a while before he answered.

'Did I wake you?' she asked.

'No. I was some distance from the phone.' His voice was deep, warm and soothing, and to hear him was a little like sipping at rich, melting chocolate. 'I was checking the rooms to see where the children might be hiding. They've taken to disappearing of a morning, and usually I manage to find them in what used to be the servants' quarters. They seem to like playing in the smaller rooms. I've never known such early birds. Where on earth do they get their energy from?'

'The fountain of youth, I should imagine.' She hesitated. 'So I take it you're still looking for them? Have you tried the kitchen?'

'I'm heading there now.' He made a soft intake of breath. 'I should have taken time to dress properly—these stone floors are cold. I need to get some carpets in here...or install under-floor heating.'

She imagined him padding barefoot over the floor, but her mind skittered away from delving any further into what he might be wearing—or not wearing, as the case may be. 'You should try living in my cottage,' she said, her tone dry. 'We don't have the luxury of central heating at the moment, since your estate manager hasn't attended to our requests for repairs, whereas you at least have the comfort of a range cooker in your kitchen, if I remember correctly.' She had ventured up to the castle in search of her errant cousin one day years ago, and the memory had stayed with her ever since.

'You're welcome to come and share it with me any time, Izzy. I think I told you that once before, but you were reluctant to take me up on the offer, as I recall. I guess you were worried about what your father might think if he found you there.' She heard a door hinge creak. 'Nope, they're not in here.'

'I expect you'll find a note on the table,' she murmured.

He was silent for a moment, taking that in, before he said on a disbelieving note, 'Are you telling me you *know* where they are?'

'That's about the size of it. Molly wanted to keep you informed.' There was a rustling of paper from the other end of the line. 'Have you found it? What does it say?'

He laughed throatily. 'Well, you're perfectly right—there are some weird hieroglyphics scrawled on a scrap of paper, if that counts. I'll see if I can decipher it.' There was a pause, and she could imagine his frown. 'Here we go, it says, "U wudnt wayk up, so we is gon down the ill to get sum fink to eet. Luv, Molly nd Camron." Brilliant.' There was a smile in his voice. 'I suppose that's not bad for a five-year-old.'

'There you are, you see. What could be clearer? The children were starving, and you were off in the land of nod, so they had to fend for themselves. Fortunately for them we were able to give them breakfast and make sure that they're warm and looked after, but I daren't think what might have happened if we hadn't been here.' She used a stern tone, but Ross was still chuckling over the note, and that served to make her crosser than ever.

'I know what you're saying,' he said, amusement threading his voice, 'and you're right, it's definitely not a good state of affairs… But you have to give them full marks for initiative, don't you? I'll come over and fetch them.'

'That would be a very good idea,' she said on

a pithy note. 'Lorna and I have to be at work in around half an hour, so if you're not here in the next few minutes we'll come and find *you*.'

She cut the call and went back to the kitchen, satisfied that at least now he would have to scoot around and get dressed, and begin to take on his responsibilities. What was he thinking of, lying in bed while the children were wandering about?

Molly and Cameron had finished eating by now, and were busy drawing pictures while Lorna collected up the breakfast dishes.

'I'll take over here if you want to go and get ready for work,' Izzy told her. 'Ross should be along to pick up the children in a few minutes.'

'He's going to take us to see Mummy today,' Molly said brightly. 'He promised.'

'And he said we'd buy some flowers for her from the shop,' Cameron added. 'He said we could choose the best flowers in the shop when we get to Inverness. She likes roses, so that's what I'm going to look for.'

'I'm sure she'll love them,' Izzy said,

'whatever you decide to buy. I'm going to see her myself tomorrow, all being well.'

She washed the breakfast dishes, leaving them to drain on the wire rack. Then she rubbed cream into her hands and checked her long hair in the mirror, clipping the chestnut waves back from her face.

Ross turned up at the house much sooner than she had expected, looking immaculate in dark chinos and a crisp shirt, and oozing vibrant energy—as though he was ready to grasp the day with both hands.

She fixed him with a smoky grey gaze. How could he possibly look like that when he'd been dead to the world not half an hour earlier? It simply wasn't fair.

'They've been waiting for you,' she said, waving him into the hallway. 'But I have to say I think you should find a way of barring the doors, so they can't simply wander off as they please. There's no knowing what they could have been up to while you were out for the count.'

He sent her an oblique glance. 'You're not going to let this go, are you? Would it help if I said the door was locked and bolted? I think Cameron climbed on a chair to retrieve the keys and unlatch the bolt.'

'Then maybe you should keep the keys closer to hand,' she said calmly. 'You should count yourself lucky that no major road passes by here.'

'I'm duly chastened,' he said, making an effort to turn down his mouth but not looking a jot sincere.

She led him into the kitchen, where the children glanced up from their drawing to acknowledge him with bright smiles.

'I've done a picture of Mummy,' Molly told him, waving her paper in the air. 'She has beautiful long hair and a pretty dress. See?'

'That's…spectacular,' he murmured, gazing down at the potato-shaped squiggle, daubed generously with a splash of bright pink crayon. 'I see you've drawn her lovely fingers, too.'

It was the right thing to say. Molly beamed with pride at her creation. The hands formed a great part of the drawing, with sausage fingers on either side, and they were her latest achievement.

Cameron, on the other hand, was tired of sitting and wanted adventure. 'When are we going to Inverness? Can we go now?'

'Soon,' Ross told him. 'I have to put a few things in a holdall first of all. We're going to meet up with your Aunt Jess at the hospital. She's come up especially from the Lake District to stay in Inverness for the next day or two, and she says she'll take you shopping as soon as you've been to see your mother. We can't have you going around looking like scruffs any longer, can we?'

Cameron shrugged, obviously not much bothered either way, while Molly looked thoughtful. Izzy guessed she was already thinking about what she would like to buy.

'Would you like a cup of tea or coffee?' Lorna asked.

Ross shook his head. 'Thanks, but I have to get a move on. Things are not going quite the way I planned this morning.' He glanced around the kitchen. 'You're having trouble with the central heating, I gather? I'll make arrangements for someone to come and deal with it.'

'That would be good,' Lorna told him. 'It's freezing in here in the mornings. And as to taking a tepid shower—I really can't recommend it.'

'No, I can imagine.' He ran his gaze over Izzy, taking in the snug fit of her jeans and the stretch material of her jersey wrap top that clung where it touched.

She had no idea what he was thinking, but Izzy's glance was frosty. 'That's not all that's wrong,' she said. 'There are roof tiles that have been missing since the high winds two or three weeks back… and part of the fence has blown down.'

He frowned. 'I didn't notice that when I drove here. Whereabouts?'

'At the side of the house.' Izzy's mouth made a crooked shape. 'I tried to fix it temporarily, with nails and a few battens, but I doubt it will hold for very long. Carpentry's not one of my skills, I'm afraid.'

Ross's gaze was thoughtful. 'I'm sure you're a woman of many talents, but obviously you shouldn't have been put in that situation. I can only say that Jake has had a lot to contend with of late, with various things happening in his family—illness and so on—or he would have seen to it.'

'I didn't realise that.' Izzy was immediately concerned. 'He didn't say.'

'No, he wouldn't. Jake's a proud man. He's probably borne the brunt of the villagers' animosity over the last few years.' He straightened, becoming brisk in his manner. 'Anyway, thanks for taking care of Molly and Cameron for me. You, too, Lorna.' His brief smile encompassed both of them. 'I'm sorry you've been troubled.'

'They've been good as gold,' Lorna told him. 'They're welcome to come and visit any time… preferably with your knowledge, of course.'

He nodded. 'I'm sure they'll want to come back fairly soon, but next time I'll make certain they call you first.'

After that Ross didn't hang around to make conversation, and Izzy wasn't sure quite how she felt about that. It wasn't really surprising that he would leave quickly. After all, she hadn't been exactly welcoming in her manner. But perhaps he also recognised that she and Lorna had to go off to work.

Anyway, after she had given each of the children a hug, he led them away and settled them in his car. He drove away without looking back.

Izzy was filled with a strange sense of unease once he had gone. She felt somehow let down, with a hollow feeling inside despite the meal, and yet, in truth, how could she have expected anything more? As things stood, she was going against the grain by even associating with him.

If her father discovered that Ross had come visiting, he'd be have been agitated in the extreme, no matter that she was perfectly entitled to run her own life the way she saw fit. That ideology hadn't stood Alice in any good stead, had it? She had been cut off from her family for several years, and was only back now because she needed specialist care and attention.

It grieved Izzy that her cousin should suffer this way. The Buchanans had a lot to answer for.

CHAPTER THREE

'ACCORDING to his wife, the man was doing a spot of sightseeing close by the falls when he slipped and fell. Luckily for him some hill walkers saw what happened and helped bring him to safety.' Greg's voice reached Izzy over the car phone. 'As far as we know he has a broken ankle and damage to his shoulder, but he's also complaining of shortness of breath. An ambulance is being sent out, but there are traffic jams on the main road causing delays, and since the tracking system shows you're nearby, with the fast response car, you may be able to reach him first.'

'Thanks, Greg.' Greg was the consultant in charge of the A&E unit where she worked, and her patient would most likely be taken into his care, unless the situation was worse than it first appeared, in which case he might have to be transferred to Inverness. 'You're right. I'm about a mile away from the gorge. I'll head straight over there.'

Izzy drove as fast as she dared, barely able to take in the wonderful scenery in this part of the Highlands. She had left Lorna back in the A&E unit. It suited Izzy to work this way—spending some of the week in the hospital setting, and the rest out and about as a first responder.

This whole area was one of outstanding natural beauty, with hills and mountains all around, thickly wooded with natural species of rowan, alder, hazel and birch. To her left, she caught glimpses of the river as it flowed downhill, disappearing every now and then as woodland obscured the view.

Before too long she came across the road junction where she had to turn off towards the falls—a place of wonder for everyone who came to visit the area. There was a narrow road leading to a car park, and from there she hoped she would be able to find the injured man without too much difficulty.

She parked the car as close as she could to the bridge, a viewpoint where people could stand and marvel at the chasm that had been carved out by glacial melt-water aeons before, and where a majestic waterfall surged downwards to the valley below. From there the water cascaded over boulders and tumbled on its course towards the sea.

The man had been carried to a small viewing platform, Izzy discovered, and as she approached she could see straight away that he was in a lot of pain and discomfort.

'Hello, Jim…and Frances,' she said, introducing herself to the patient and his wife. 'I'm Dr McKinnon.' She knelt down beside the man, who was sitting propped up against the metal guardrail. 'The ambulance is on its way, but I'll take a look at you and see what I can do to make you more comfortable in the meantime, if I may?'

Jim nodded. He tried to speak, but he was struggling to get his breath, and Izzy could see that there was a film of sweat on his brow. He looked anxious, his features strained and desperate, as was the case with many seriously ill people that Izzy had come across.

'I can see that your ankle is swollen and your shoulder appears to be dislocated,' she said. 'Do you have pain anywhere else?'

Jim used his good arm to slope a finger towards his chest. 'Hurts to…breathe,' he said.

'The pain came on before he fell,' his wife put in. 'He started to cough, and then it seemed as though he was going to pass out. Is it his heart, do you think?'

'I'll listen to his chest and see if I can find out what's going on,' Izzy said. 'Have you had any heart problems before this, Jim?'

He shook his head and she gave her patient a reassuring smile. 'Try not to worry,' she said. 'We'll sort it all out. For now, I'm going to give you oxygen to help you to breathe, and I'll give you an injection to ease the pain.'

Izzy placed the oxygen mask over his mouth and nose and checked that the flow of oxygen was adequate. Then she listened carefully to his chest.

'Did you have any other symptoms before

the chest pain?' she asked. 'Even up to a day or so before?'

Jim frowned, trying to think about that, but his pain was obviously getting the better of him, and as he started to shake his head once more his wife put in, 'He said his leg was sore. Apart from that he was fine. We've just come back from a trip to New Zealand. This was a final weekend break before we go back home and start getting ready for Christmas.'

'Hmm.' Izzy was thoughtful. 'We need to do tests to be certain what's causing your problems, Jim, but it could be that a blood clot is blocking the circulation to your lungs. I'm going to give you medication to stop any clots forming and ease the blood flow, and then we'll concentrate on getting you to hospital as soon as possible.'

Izzy set up an intravenous line so that she could give him anticoagulant and painkilling medication as necessary. Then she moved away from the couple momentarily, to use her mobile phone and call the ambulance services.

'How long is the ambulance likely to be?' she

asked. 'I need to have this patient transported urgently to hospital. I think he may be suffering from a pulmonary embolism, and I don't believe we have any time to lose.'

'Okay. Leave it with us,' the controller said. 'There's a problem with the ambulance, but we'll get someone to you as soon as possible.'

Izzy turned back to her patient and contemplated his other injuries. 'I'm pretty sure your ankle is broken,' she told him, 'so I'll immobilise that in a splint. As to the shoulder, the same thing applies. I'll secure it for you in the most comfortable position, and then the hospital team will put it back in place for you while you're under anaesthetic.'

She worked quickly to do that, all the while looking out for the ambulance. Her patient was most likely suffering from a blood clot that had passed from his leg to his lung, and she was conscious that if it was not treated quickly his life could be at risk.

'How are you feeling now?' she asked him.

'It's better now that the pain has gone,' he said,

but she could see that he was still struggling to breathe. She glanced around, but there was still no sign of the ambulance. Her gaze rested momentarily on the majestic scenery of the gorge. Trees and ferns sprang from clefts and fissures in the rock, and above everything was the gentle sound of rushing water. It was such a glorious, peaceful scene that it seemed incongruous that she was here trying to save someone's life.

Then came a humming sound from overhead, like the drone of insects coming ever closer, until at last the noise was all around and an air ambulance helicopter hovered, preparing to land, its rotors spinning, fanning the air like giant flapping wings.

'Is that for us?' Frances asked, and Izzy nodded. 'It looks that way.' She glanced at Jim. 'They'll take you to Inverness,' she told him. 'At least with the helicopter you should be there within minutes.'

The helicopter came to rest some distance away, on a flat stretch of ground near to the car park, and a medic jumped down, followed by a paramedic.

Between them they wheeled a trolley towards Izzy and her patient, and as she watched them draw near she made a sudden, swift intake of breath.

Surely that was Ross in the medic's uniform? What was *he* doing here? Of course she knew that he had trained as a doctor, but his work had always been in the Lake District. This had to be new, this job working with the air ambulance.

As he approached she did her best to get over the shock and try to recover her professionalism. Her patient must come first. Any questions she might want to fire at him could surely be answered later?

'Hello, how are you doing?' Ross said, coming over to the group assembled on the viewing platform and checking on the patient. He glanced at Izzy. 'Hi,' he said. 'Ambulance control told me you were the doctor on call.' Then he concentrated his attention on the patient once more. 'You collapsed, I understand, and injured yourself?'

Jim nodded, unable to speak just then, and Izzy began to explain the situation. 'He has severe chest pain and difficulty breathing, as well as a broken ankle and dislocated shoulder.' She went on to outline her diagnosis and explain what medication she had given him. 'He'll need to go for an urgent angiography, and I suspect he'll require thrombolytic therapy in order to break down any clot that's formed.'

He nodded. 'I'll alert Radiology back at Inverness. They have all the facilities there. And I'll notify the cardiovascular surgeon to be on hand to perform the surgery if necessary.'

All the time they were talking, they were breaking off to reassure Jim that everything was being done that should be done, and preparing him for transfer to the trolley. 'We'll have you secure in no time,' Ross told him. 'I can see Dr McKinnon has been taking good care of you. No worries. You're in good hands.'

They worked quickly to strap their patient safely in place, covering him with a blanket to keep him warm and prevent shock. Ross glanced at Frances. 'Will you be coming along with us? We can find room for you in the 'copter if you like.'

'Thank you. I'd like that. I want to stay with him.'

'Good.' Ross and the paramedic started to walk with the trolley towards the waiting helicopter. Izzy accompanied them, keeping a check on her patient's vital signs.

She glanced towards Ross. 'I had no idea you had taken a job with the air ambulance,' she said in a low voice.

'The opportunity came up, and it seemed too good a chance to miss,' he answered. 'They needed someone to fill in for one of the doctors who was away for a couple of months, and with Alice likely to be in the hospital for the next few weeks it looked as though the job was tailor-made for me.'

'What happened to your work in the Lake District?'

'My contract came to an end. They'll hold it open for me in case I decide to go back next year on a permanent basis, but I thought with Jake leaving it was time for me to come and take up the reins of the estate for a while.'

She studied him as they lifted the trolley bed on to the aircraft. So there was still the possibility that he wasn't going to be staying around. Why didn't that come as any real surprise to her?

'I'm even more startled to see you here today, right now,' she murmured, going into the medical bay of the helicopter. 'It was only this morning that you and the children were heading off to Inverness. What happened to your plans to go and see Alice?'

He gave a brief smile. 'Oh, we did all that. Afterwards I left them with their aunt Jess, so that I could come in to work. She's going to keep them with her in Inverness for a couple of days. At the moment things are a little tricky for me because of the shift system I'm working, but I dare say it will all work out in the end.'

The paramedic made sure that the trolley bed was locked in place and that Frances was happily settled close by her husband's side. Then he came over to Izzy and Ross. He must have heard what they were saying because he commented, 'In fact, Ross and I had a difficult stint last night. We didn't get finished until after midnight. There was a boy injured and lost on the hills, and being pitch-black out there it took us a while to find him. He was okay, as it turned out—just a little shaken up and suffering from exposure and a pulled ligament in his knee.'

'Oh, I see.' That explained why Molly had found it difficult to wake Ross this morning. Izzy felt a wave of guilt wash over her. Had she been too quick to pass judgement on him?

She checked the intravenous line and made sure that Jim was comfortable. He was struggling to take in oxygen through the breathing mask, and she settled it more comfortably over his face. 'You'll be in hospital in no time at all,' she told him. 'The doctors will do a scan to see if there's a clot on your lung. If they find one, they could decide to go on treating you with medication, or they may want to remove it using a thin catheter threaded through the blood vessel. Either way, you will be well looked after.'

She said goodbye to Jim and his wife and went

to the open door of the helicopter. Ross went with her, jumping down to the ground and reaching up to help her descend. His hands went around her waist, his palms lying flat on her ribcage as he lifted her down with ease, as though she was as light as a feather.

When her feet touched the ground his hands stayed on her, as though he would steady her, and she realised with a slight sense of shock that her own fingers still lay on his shoulders. Her whole body responded as though he had triggered an electric current.

Coming to her senses, she drew back her fingers, her mind skittering with uncertainty.

'So that's why you were lying in bed this morning,' she murmured. 'I have to take back all the bad things I was thinking.' She frowned. 'Only, who was watching over the children last night if you were out working?'

'You were thinking bad things?' His mouth made a flattened shape. 'I thought as much.' He straightened, letting his hands fall away from her. 'You don't trust me at all, do you?'

'Put it down to the fall out from times gone by,' she murmured.

He gave a faint smile. 'As always. Actually, I did have things all in hand. I arranged for Maggie to stay and watch over them until I returned home. She was pleased enough to do it. Of course I'll have to organise things a little better if I'm to stay for a while. Molly and Cameron need some kind of stability, and getting them enrolled in school is going to be one of the first things I must do.'

'Yes, that's probably best.' Izzy stepped away from the vehicle. 'I should let you go,' she said softly. This was neither the time nor the place to be holding a conversation about his future plans, much as her curiosity was pricked. Wind from the helicopter's rotors tousled her hair, and she lifted a hand to hold the strands away from her face. 'If you get the chance, let me know how our patient progresses, will you?'

He nodded. 'I will. You can count on it.'

She moved away, and he slid the door of the helicopter shut. Within moments the aircraft rose skywards and zoomed away.

Watching the helicopter move out of sight, Izzy was assailed by a strange notion of unfinished business. Seeing Ross at work had given her a tremendous jolt, and along with it had come the realisation that their paths might cross much more often than she had ever expected.

Today had not been a good start. Why hadn't she guarded her tongue instead of alerting him to all her doubts and criticisms? He was simply doing a job, making the best of things just as she was, and it was wrong of her to find fault with everything he did. It was in his favour that he was taking care of the children at all. Perhaps she should leave it to her father to cast aspersions on his motives.

Her father, as things turned out, was in a highly charged mood when she visited him later that day.

'You're working with Ross Buchanan?' His tone was grim. 'As if it isn't bad enough that he's back among us. Why do we have to rub shoulders with him, too?'

Izzy's mother came into the living room, setting down the tea tray on a low coffee table.

She glanced at Izzy. 'Sit yourself down, love. You've had a trying day by all accounts. You should relax with a cup of tea and some cake. I had a baking session this morning—fruitcake. Help yourself.' She shook her head, making the soft brown tendrils of hair quiver as she lifted the teapot. 'You wouldn't think so many people would manage to get themselves into difficulties up in the hills, would you?'

Izzy sat down on the sofa and leaned forward to slide a wedge of cake on to a plate. 'I'm more surprised that there are so many people who still want to walk the hills in December,' she murmured. She glanced at her father. 'As to Ross, he is at least doing a worthwhile job. You have to grant him that, surely?'

'I'll not grant him anything,' her father said gruffly. 'I've heard that he's brought builders in to go on with that log cabin project his father started on the estate some six years back. I don't know how on earth he managed to get planning permission. A lot of people objected to the development, and from my point of view it'll be certain to draw away the tourists. I'm sure that's his grand plan.'

'But you'll be all right, won't you?' Izzy said. 'You have the regular people who come every year for the fishing. That's more than a lot of the villagers have.'

'That's only because I kept hold of this land and my father and his father before him fought to stay on it. There were no thanks due to the old Laird and the generations that followed him for that. Their land borders ours, and if they'd had their way they'd have long since moved the boundaries and made it their own.'

Izzy bit into her cake and tried to keep exasperation from getting the better of her. She had learnt long ago that there was no point in arguing with her father when he was in this frame of mind.

Her mother's gaze met hers across the table. 'Your father's upset because the salmon fishing went awry this year. There's something wrong with the stretch of the river that flows across our land. He reckons it's to do with some changes the

Laird made higher up, at a point before the river reaches us.'

'But Ross wasn't here when all that went on, was he?' Izzy murmured. 'I don't see how he can be to blame for everything that goes wrong around here.'

Her father's brows shot up. 'So who do you think gave Jake his instructions? And that log cabin has been a sore point for a long time. Not just the cabin, but the lodges that go along with it. He said it was just for living accommodation for the family, but what does he need with that when he has the castle? Draughty it might be, and in need of repair, but they've lived there for generations without needing any cabins or lodges. It's just an excuse. He'll lure away the tourists to line his own pockets and take away any chance we have of making a living.'

'He may not be here for all that long,' Izzy said, accepting a cup of tea from her mother and taking slow sips of the hot liquid. 'He said something about his job being kept open for him back in the Lake District. I have the feeling that he's here to make sure Alice is going to be all right and to allow the children to be with her. Perhaps he's planning on taking them all home once she's well again.'

She frowned, thinking things over. Ross had always had a soft spot for Alice. If his brother hadn't swept her away from him, who knew what might have come of their relationship? Perhaps Alice was bound to turn to him now more than ever. How would Ross react to that? Would he be pleased? Why else was he staying around to look after her when she had her older sister, Jess, to care for her?

It wasn't something that she wanted to dwell on. Thinking about Ross and Alice as a couple always had the power to upset her. Her own feelings towards him were unsettling, and had caused her many a sleepless night. She put down her cup and brushed crumbs from her lap.

'Are you all right?' her mother asked. Grey eyes studied her thoughtfully.

'I'm fine.' Izzy gave her mother a reassuring smile. She didn't want to confide in her about the way her thoughts had turned, especially with her father looking on. Instead, she murmured, 'I suppose I was thinking about Alice. It must be difficult for her, coming back here after all this time and yet still being so far away from her roots. Anyway, I'm going to see her tomorrow after work, all being well. You're welcome to come along with me, if you like.'

She was aware of her father's sharp glance resting on her as she spoke, but this was one instance where she would not back down. Alice had been like a sister to her, and the children, likewise, were precious to her…to Ross, too, if the truth were known.

'I'd like that,' her mother said. She shot a look over to her husband. 'Alice is family,' she said, 'and you have to agree that she's had more than her fair share of bad luck. Are you not going to come along with us and make your peace with her?'

Izzy's father stood up abruptly. 'You know how I feel about the situation,' he said, his tone brisk. 'Alice left of her own accord. She knew full well what she was doing when she chose to go off with a Buchanan.'

'But the bairns, Stuart. Think of the bairns. Do you have no compassion?' Her mother's gaze entreated him. 'What have they ever done to deserve being outcast?'

'You go and see her and look to the bairns,' he said. 'I have things to do. I have to make repairs and get the boat ready for next season—or there'll be no trips for the sea fishing and our income will take another dive. We have to do something to counteract the actions of our neighbours.'

He walked out of the room, his back straight, his head held high, and Izzy gave a soft sigh.

'No one could say that you didn't try, Mum,' she said.

'For all the good it did me.' Her mother poured more tea. 'You know he thinks Ross had something to do with causing the accident, don't you? He's battling with himself over that. He's trying to come to terms with what happened to Alice, but he's incensed because Ross might have had something to do with it.'

'I don't understand.' Izzy sat bolt upright, a line indenting her brow. 'How could Ross have had anything to do with the car smash? I heard he was hurt and had to be hospitalised with a chest injury.'

'He was following them. Robert and Alice were driving over to her sister's house to pick up the children, from what I heard. Ross was on the same road, and rumour has it that they'd all argued over something and feelings were running high. Folk say it was because she always cared for Ross, and Robert resented that. They think Robert lost control of the car because Ross was edging closer. Robert tried to pick up speed to outrun him, and then he took a bend too wide and it ended up as a three-car smash. It's a wonder no one else was killed.'

Izzy was stunned by that revelation. 'Perhaps it's just that—as you say, rumour. If Ross had been driving dangerously the police would have prosecuted him, wouldn't they?'

'There was no proof. It was summertime, and the roads were dry. There doesn't seem to be any other reason for the accident.'

Izzy shook her head. 'I don't believe it,' she said.

'I don't believe Ross would have done anything to jeopardise the safety of his brother or Alice.'

Her mother laid a hand on her shoulder. 'I only told you because I don't want you to be hurt,' she said. 'You try to look for the good in people, but the Buchanans have always brought trouble. Your father takes a stance that is hard to understand sometimes, but he's protective of his family, and he was hurt when Alice ran away. To him it was like a betrayal, and the Buchanans were at the centre of it.'

Izzy understood that well enough. She just had no idea where all this bad feeling would lead. Nowhere good, that was for sure.

CHAPTER FOUR

'UNCLE ROSS, Izzy says she's going to do some baking,' Molly exclaimed eagerly, tugging at Ross's trousers. 'We want to stay and help her. Can we? She said we could if you thought it was all right.'

Ross frowned. He was standing by his Range Rover, outside Izzy's cottage, preparing to open up the door to the car's loading area. 'I don't see how we can do that today,' he murmured. 'I have to go back home and talk to the men who are doing some building work for me. I'm sorry. Perhaps another time.'

Molly's face crumpled. 'Oh, but she's making gingerbread men for the Christmas sale.'

'They're going to switch on the Christmas lights in the village tomorrow,' Cameron put in. 'Maggie said so. We wanted to make something for the stalls. Lorna said she'd ask if she and Izzy could take us to look around. They have all sorts of toys on sale. We could spend our pocket money.'

'Whoa…steady on a minute.' Ross threw up his hands as though to ward off the two youngsters. 'This has jumped a bit, hasn't it, from me dropping off a couple of heaters for Izzy? Now I'm being roped in for baking sessions and an outing to the Christmas lights ceremony. I hadn't bargained for any of that.'

Cameron put on his best angelic expression. 'Mum *always* takes us to see the Christmas lights back home,' he said, emphasising his words carefully. 'She says it's *magical* and singing Christmas carols round the tree is the start of all the celebrations.'

'And she can't go this year, so we could go for her and find her a present,' Molly added, sealing the argument. 'It would cheer her up no end to have some presents if she's going to be in hospital at Christmas.'

Ross rolled his eyes heavenwards. 'If I didn't

know better I'd say you had this all planned out beforehand. Have you two been making deals with Izzy and Lorna?'

'No.' Molly and Cameron both made wide, innocent eyes, and even Izzy, who *did* know better, would have been fooled—except for Molly's soft-spoken admission. 'But we were at the shop with Maggie, and Izzy's mother said it was a nice idea, and Mr McKinnon said, "That would bring him down from his ivory tower, wouldn't it?" I didn't really understand that bit.' She frowned. 'Perhaps he meant Santa would be there?' She sent her uncle a quizzical look, while his face in turn took on a faintly stunned expression, his head going back a fraction, as though she'd just poked him in the eye.

Molly's gaze was uncertain now, and Izzy groaned inwardly, pulling a face. Turning away so that the children wouldn't see, she said in a soft plea, 'Ross, you don't have to take my father's words at face value. He's not himself lately, with Alice being in hospital and his summer season going badly. He's not approaching anything with a good frame of mind.'

'Oh, I don't know about that.' Ross's mouth made a flat line. 'I think your father's pretty much living up to expectations.' He looked down at Molly and Cameron. 'So, you think Santa might be there, do you?'

Molly nodded. 'He's going to have a grotto at the back of the community hall. That's what Mary said, up at the shop. She said it would be a treat for us to go and see him.'

'Hmm.' He studied his niece and nephew thoughtfully. 'I think I'm beginning to see a conspiracy at work here. You do realise that I might have to work tomorrow evening, don't you? I'm on call, and I may not be able to stay with you, which means Maggie will be in charge.'

'She won't mind if Izzy and Lorna say they'll look after us,' Cameron put in quickly, sensing that his uncle might be weakening.

Ross's mouth twisted at that, but he glanced towards Izzy with slightly raised eyebrows. 'Are you sure about all this? Do you know what you're letting yourselves in for?'

'I'm okay with it,' Izzy said, 'and Lorna's

game, too. I'll keep in touch with Maggie, if you like, to let her know what's going on. And as for the baking—well, I could bring the children back to you as soon as we're done. I'm assuming you'll be at home later this afternoon?'

He nodded. 'I'll be showing the builders round the place. There are a few things that need doing—improving the damp course and pointing up the walls. I have to somehow try to turn the place into a home. I think Molly and Cameron are finding it a bit draughty and cold, especially in their bedrooms. They've been used to all their home comforts back in the Lake District. Which led me to thinking about your problems... I thought maybe you would be able to make use of these oil-filled radiators.'

He opened up the back of his car to reveal two mobile heaters stacked in the back. 'I've asked an engineer to come and have a look at your central heating system, but he's planned on coming along on Monday. I don't know if that will be a problem for you.'

'I'll be on duty at the hospital on Monday,'

Izzy said, thinking things through. 'It's my on-call day. I'm not sure whether Lorna will be here to show him around.'

'No problem,' Lorna put in. 'It's my day off.' She grinned mischievously. 'There's no chance he'll be single, as well as tall, dark and handsome, I suppose?'

Ross chuckled. 'That depends very much on your viewpoint, I imagine. He seems okay to me, but who am I to judge? As far as I know he isn't accounted for.'

'That's sorted, then. His goose is as good as cooked.' Lorna peered into the car. 'Oh, they look just the business, don't they? And each of them big enough to heat a large room. They'll retain the heat for a while, as well, being oil filled. Great.'

'I'm glad I could help.' Ross lifted out the heaters and started to carry them into the cottage. 'I've arranged for someone else to come and look at the roof, but the fence will take a little longer to put right. The carpenter has a full work-load after all the damage caused by the storm, but he'll come and sort it out as soon as possible.'

'That's okay. At least we know that repairs are in hand.' Izzy showed him where to place the heaters on the floor of the kitchen. 'Thanks for dealing with it so speedily.'

'It's the least I can do.' He made a crooked smile. 'Besides, I wouldn't want to give your father any more ammunition to fire at me. Last I heard he was calling a meeting with the villagers to hatch a protest over the building work on the estate.'

Izzy wasn't sure how to respond to that. Her father had every reason to worry about the effect Ross's plans would have on his own tourist bookings, but as far as she could tell Ross was within his rights to go ahead with the work—unless he had extended the remit of the plans.

He bent to say goodbye to the children. 'Be good, both of you…and if you get the chance save a gingerbread man for your mother. We could take it over to her tomorrow morning.'

Molly and Cameron whooped with excitement, before going off with Lorna to wash their hands.

Izzy walked with him back to the car. 'I wish

you and my father would try to call a truce,' she said. 'Could you not arrange a meeting of your own and try to iron out a few of the problems between you?'

He laid a hand on his chest, as though she had knocked him for six. 'Do you really believe there's any chance that he would agree to it?' He shook his head. 'Living in cloud cuckoo land springs to mind.'

He walked round to the driver's side of the car and pulled open the door. 'I don't blame you for trying, though, Izzy…ever the peace-maker. Only I think you underestimate the extent of the problem.'

He smiled. 'I promise for my part that I'll try to keep things on a civil footing, but I have to bring the estate into the twenty-first century, and that means taking steps that may not be popular with everyone.' Sliding into his seat, he added, 'Will you give me a ring when you're bringing the children back? That way I'll make sure I'm able to greet you at the main door.'

She nodded, watching him as he drove away.

Her thoughts were troubled as she went back to the kitchen, but the children were waiting and she put on a bright smile.

'All right, then,' she said, looking at them. 'What's the first thing we do when we're about to bake?'

'Weigh out the flour?' Molly suggested.

'That's certainly something we need to do, but not the first thing. Good try, but no.'

'Wash our hands?' Cameron said, holding his up for her to see.

'Another good answer, but not quite what I was thinking.' She went over to the cooker. 'We switch on the oven so that it can be heating up while we mix the ingredients. See?' She turned the dial. 'Right, then. Where's Lorna? I thought she was going to help us?'

'I'm here,' Lorna said, coming into the kitchen. 'I'm hungry already, just at the thought of baking. Shall we make some chocolate butterfly cakes, as well?'

An hour or so later they were all flour spattered, and a wonderful aroma of chocolate and ginger filled the kitchen. Molly and Cameron had smears of chocolate around their mouths, and Molly was putting the finishing touches to the icing on the last of the gingerbread men.

'That one's for Mummy,' she said, 'and this one's for Uncle Ross. Do you think he'll like his green icing tie?'

'He'll love it,' Lorna answered. 'He's definitely the best-looking gingerbread man in the bunch.'

A short time later the children went up to the bathroom to clean up, while Izzy and Lorna tidied the kitchen.

'They're desperately hoping that Alice will be well enough to come home in the New Year,' Lorna said. 'Do you think it will happen?'

'I'm not sure,' Izzy said with a frown. 'She's still very weak, but the physiotherapist is coming in every day to work with her, and Greg is keeping an eye on things on the days when he's based at the hospital in Inverness.' She rinsed the baking tray and placed it on the rack on the draining board. 'The one thing she has in her favour is that she's desperate to get back home to be with the children. She's worried about how they're settling. They've been through a lot of upheaval in the last few months.'

Lorna nodded. 'It must make her feel better to know that you're keeping an eye on them. Ross seems to be doing everything within his means, but you're family, too, and they probably need that extra involvement.'

Izzy washed the pastry board, thinking about the time she had spent with her cousin in hospital. 'Alice has asked me to keep track of how they're doing—I would have done it anyway, because I think the world of Molly and Cameron. She knows Ross will do his very best for them, but she's aware of how the villagers feel about the Buchanans, and she doesn't know if any of that will rub off on the children. Once they start to go to school here there might be problems, and added to that Ross is a busy man, with lots of demands on his time and energy. She worries that they might be missing out on love and cuddles.'

'There's not much chance of that,' Lorna said

with a smile, drying the mixing bowl with a teatowel. 'Every time they come round you give them a big hug, and from what I hear Alice does the same at every visit.'

Molly and Cameron came into the room, arguing noisily. '*I'm* giving Mummy the chocolate cake with icing on it,' Molly said in an emphatic tone. 'You're giving her the one with the butterfly wings.'

'I want to give her one with icing,' Cameron insisted. 'I said it first.'

'You could both give her one of each *and* a gingerbread man,' Izzy said, cutting in. 'That way she'll have a treat for nearly every day of the week.'

Satisfied, the children accepted that compromise, and some time later Izzy set off with them along the path to Ross's home, taking with her a couple of rugs from the attic that might go well in the children's rooms.

The castle was a grand stone building, with a square turret and long rectangular windows. It was situated towards the end of a long, rocky promontory, almost an island in itself, where the waters of the loch lapped gently against the craggy shoreline.

From some distance away the sea washed into the loch, and depending on the tide part of the land leading to the promontory might be flooded with water. A wide stone bridge spanned this stretch of land between the mainland and the castle, and Izzy paused there for a moment to gaze at Ross's Highland home. It was beautiful, golden in the dying sunlight of the December day, a majestic edifice set against the clear blue of the sky, with a backdrop of wooded hills and distant mountain peaks and the glassy surface of the loch all around.

Ross met her at the main door, as promised, and immediately Molly bombarded him with the delights of her baking session. 'I've made you a gingerbread man,' she said, 'and Cameron's made you a chocolate cake.'

'Just what I wanted,' he said, ushering the children into the large hall and turning to relieve Izzy of the parcels she was carrying. 'Here, let me help,' he said, placing them down on an elegant side-table.

He laid a hand lightly on the small of her back. 'Come in, Izzy. It must be years since you've been up here. Will you stay awhile and have a drink with me? I can offer you tea, coffee, or something stronger... A glass of mulled wine, maybe, or perhaps you'd like to try one of our special fruit wines?'

'Well...I ought to go back and give Lorna a hand with the chores,' she said in a diffident fashion, wanting to back out, but searching for an excuse. It was one thing to watch over the children, or meet up with Ross because of their work commitments, but it was quite another to deliberately fraternise with the enemy.

She hadn't bargained on the intimacy of his touch, though. It undermined all her defences. He was only welcoming her into his home, but his greeting felt very much like a caress. Even now it was doing strange things to her nervous system, so that all her senses had erupted into a feverish flurry of excitement.

'I...um...I just wanted to drop off these wool rugs,' she told him, indicating the parcels. 'My aunt gave them to me when I moved into the cottage, but I've never had occasion to use them since my mother also gave me some. I thought they might come in handy for the children, though. They said the floors were bare in their rooms, and it might be nice for them to have them at the side of their beds. They're very colourful, and they seem to like them, so it's a shame for them to stay up in my attic. Unless you object, that is?'

'I think it's a great idea. It saves me wondering what to put down for them.' He smiled. 'The chores will wait for a while, won't they? I know you've been in to work this morning, and now you've had a busy afternoon, so I'm sure you could do with a break. Let me show you around.' He let his hand fall from her, and with that action her head began to clear a little.

'Shall I take your jacket?' he asked. 'I'll hang it up for you.'

She gave in, curiosity about the house overcoming her reluctance to linger and be lured into his silken trap. 'All right, I'll stay for just a little while.' She shrugged out of her jacket and he went to put it on a hanger in the cloakroom, then fetched the rugs from the table.

'Maggie left a ham and some cheeses out on the table in the kitchen,' he said, 'and we could share some of her fresh-baked bread if you've a mind to. I haven't eaten yet, and I could do with a snack. I expect the children could, too—unless they've filled up on cakes and cookies.'

As he spoke he led the way through the wide oak-panelled hall into the drawing room. Light flooded in here through windows that were almost floor-to-ceiling, casting a gentle late-afternoon glow over everything. Across the room there was an oak beam fireplace, where glowing coals in the grate sparked yellow flames, giving out warmth that filled the room. The furniture was luxurious, with deep-cushioned sofas and armchairs upholstered in light-coloured plush fabrics, and Izzy saw that there was a lovely Sheraton writing table to one side, along with a bookcase made of the same beautifully polished rosewood.

'That sounds tempting,' she said, 'but I think

you'll find Molly and Cameron are stuffed to the gills. They tried a little of everything as we went along.'

'You didn't?'

She shook her head. 'Lorna is the one who likes cakes and buns and biscuits. She's lucky. She can eat anything and not put on an ounce of weight.'

He studied her, his gaze shimmering over the clinging lines of her cotton top and smooth denim jeans. 'I don't believe for one minute that *you* have a problem on that score.'

A flush of heat ran along her cheekbones, and to distract him from the subject, she gazed around. 'This is a beautiful room,' she murmured. 'Is it your doing? I don't remember it from when I was here last.'

He nodded. 'I organised the renovation when I was here on one of my brief visits. I aim to improve the whole building—even if I have to do it one room at a time. In fact, I could show you the rooms where the children are sleeping. Maybe you could give me some advice on how to change the decor in there. I was thinking about laying down carpets, but in the meantime the rugs you've brought will be very useful.'

'I could do that,' she said carefully. After all, Alice had asked her to keep an eye on the children, hadn't she? 'I expect it's been difficult for you, figuring out what's best for Molly and Cameron?'

'You're right. It hasn't been easy. Though of course I did have contact with them before the accident. I used to visit my brother and Alice whenever it was possible. But my work took me around and about, so it wasn't possible to see them on a regular basis.'

He looked around. 'The children seem to have disappeared. I expect they've gone to play in their rooms.' Childish voices from a short distance away seemed to confirm that, and he said, 'Shall we take the rugs up there?'

She nodded. 'That might be a good idea.'

'I know Alice worries about how the children are getting on,' he said, 'and I've tried to reassure her. But if you see how things really are, you might be able to set her mind at rest.'

'I'm sure Alice appreciates everything that

you're doing for her and for the children,' Izzy said. 'She told me how marvellous you've been, helping ever since the accident.'

'I couldn't stand by and do nothing, could I? Robert was my brother, after all, and Molly and Cameron are his children. As for Alice—I've always looked out for her.'

They went back to the hall and started up the stairs. Izzy said carefully, 'Is that why you came back here—to bring Alice closer to her family? After all, you could have found a hospital nearer to where you were living, couldn't you? Up until now you've never shown any interest in coming back here to stay for any length of time.'

He sent her an oblique glance. 'That was part of it. I knew that she would want to be near to you and your mother, and it was difficult for both of you to visit as often as you would have liked while she was in the Lake District.'

'And the other part?'

He made a brief smile. 'That's a little more complicated. I was always conscious of the need to deal with the estate, and I'd been thinking about moving back here for some time. But I was always busy with my work. I enjoyed what I was doing, and I had no real reason to come back to this place while Jake was looking after things. As far as I was concerned it was being managed well enough with my input from a distance.'

He paused at the top of the stairs, looking around. 'I knew this was what my brother had always wanted. I offered him the chance to take over, to run the estate, but Robert wouldn't consider it. He saw it as second best. If he couldn't be the true Laird, he didn't want any part of it.'

'I'm sorry. That must have been difficult for you.'

'Maybe a little. It stuck in his throat that I had the inheritance but didn't have any inclination to take it up wholeheartedly. It caused more than a few problems between us, though in the end he and Alice decided that they *would* come back home to Glenmuir. I think they were hoping that they might eventually put things right with your father, and Robert was planning to develop his business interests back here. I'd have been happy for him to live at the castle, but he wouldn't take me up on it.'

She studied him, taking in his tall, proud stance. He wouldn't bend under pressure, nor would he simply do what he felt other people expected of him, but he'd cared deeply for his brother, and surely his actions showed that he felt the same about Alice? He still hadn't properly answered her question, though, had he? Why was he *really* here now, setting up a home for his brother's children? Was it purely for love of Alice? Just how strong were his feelings for her?

Her mind skittered. Maybe deep down she didn't want to know the answer to that. Already she had a leaden feeling in her stomach, as though she was weighed down by the possibility that Alice meant everything to him.

He walked across the wide landing and pushed open a heavy wooden door. 'This is Cameron's room,' he said. 'Perhaps he'd like to have the dark blue rug in here. It would certainly blend in with the decor.'

Cameron was sitting on the wooden floor, playing with his toy soldiers, lining them up on the battlements of a wooden fort, but he looked up as Izzy and Ross entered the room. 'Is that for me?' he said, breaking off to give a sudden sneeze, and looking pleased as Ross laid the rug down beside him.

Ross nodded, 'Izzy thought you might like it.' He looked closely at the boy. 'Are you warm enough? You sound as though you're coming down with a cold.'

Cameron nodded and sneezed again. 'It's better now that you've put the heater in here.'

'Good.' Ross glanced around. 'I thought Izzy might know how to brighten the room up a bit for you. I'm not exactly sure what you'd want in here.'

'An outer-space duvet,' Cameron said. 'Or a pirate one. And a table where I can do my drawing. That would be good.'

Izzy smiled. 'There's a boy who knows what he wants. Perhaps matching curtains, and a cushion or two with some of the colours picked out from the duvet and the rug would make it cosy?' She looked around the large square room. 'I expect a treasure chest would be just the thing for toys, and an upholstered wooden bench-type seat would fit in with the furnishing throughout the house.'

'I think we have both of those in one of the old servants' rooms,' Ross commented, a thoughtful look coming into his eyes. 'I'm not sure at the moment whether we have a suitable table, but I could find something in the antique shops, I dare say.'

'It doesn't have to be a table,' Izzy murmured. 'What about a small writing desk and a set of bookshelves? I imagine you must have those somewhere in the house?'

His mouth curved. 'You're right—we do. There's a child-size desk in the study, and we have lots of bookcases around the place.' He sent Cameron a questioning look. 'How does all that sound to you?'

'Pretty good,' Cameron acknowledged, losing interest and turning back to his toy soldiers. As Izzy and Ross left the room he was imitating the sound of gunfire, and several of the 'enemy' were being knocked to the ground.

'That's Cameron sorted. One more to go,' Ross murmured as they headed towards Molly's room next door. 'I wonder if she'll be as easy to please?'

'Pink,' Molly said a moment later, when Ross asked how she'd like her room to be decorated. 'Lots of pink.' She had been playing with the dolls in her dolls' house, but for now she seemed content to put them to one side.

'Ahh.' Ross tried to disguise a wince, and Izzy smiled.

'We can do pink, can't we?' she said, giving his ankle a nudge with her foot.

'Um…yes. I'm sure we'll be able to come up with something along those lines.' He looked to Izzy for support, his dark brows lifting a fraction, as though to say, *You're not serious?*

'Pink is good,' Izzy said, looking around. 'I can imagine dusky pink seating, pale rosewood furniture, and a pretty screen in the corner decorated with delicate flowers and leaves. And what about a touch of dove-grey in the curtains and bedspread? That would go really well with the rug, wouldn't it?'

Molly nodded vigorously. 'And that lovely pink-covered box seat from the big bedroom would be perfect in here.' She frowned. 'But Maggie said it was being used for blankets.'

'You mean the ottoman?' Ross queried. When Molly looked confused, he said, 'The big box at the end of the bed? In the room across the hall?'

'Yes, that's the one. It has little wooden arms either side and I love it.' Molly's eyes widened in expectation. 'Could I have it for my toys, and for a seat? The blankets could go somewhere else, couldn't they? *Please?*'

'I don't see any reason why not.' He gazed down at her. 'Anything else?'

She shook her head so that her curls quivered. 'No, thank you. I'm going to play now, if that's all right?'

Ross reached down and tousled her silky hair. 'That's fine, poppet. I'll be downstairs with Izzy if you need me.'

He led the way along the landing and down

the stairs. 'Shall we go through to the kitchen?' he suggested.

'Okay.' She followed as he led the way. 'Just for a few minutes, though. As I said, I shouldn't stay too long.' It would be all too easy to get carried away, wandering through the rooms of this fascinating building. It was far different from what she remembered, and that must be on account of Ross's renovations over the years. For all that he had asked for her help, he seemed already to have a sure touch when it came to creating a luxurious, yet comfortable home.

'Of course—just as you like. I imagine you've had quite enough for one day and could do with some relaxation.' Sending her a fleeting glance, he asked, 'How is it that you came to be working this morning, anyway? I thought you had the weekends off?'

'I do, mostly. This is my weekend on call with the Mountain Rescue team, though. We had to go and help a woman who slipped and fell while she was out walking. She took a tumble down a slope and landed on rocky ground. I think she'll be all right, but she broke her leg and had to be stretch-ered back to the ambulance. It was lucky for her that we found her reasonably quickly. I gave her pain medication and managed to stem the bleeding before we took her back to our A&E unit.' Her mouth made a downward curve. 'I don't think she's having a very good end to this year, but maybe she'll be on the mend by the time the new one comes in.'

'Let's hope so. It's interesting that you go out with the team,' he said. 'I had a call from the Mountain Rescue chief the other day, asking if I'd like to join them. He remembered that I had some experience of rescue work. I said I'd think about it, depending on how much time I would have to put in and whether I could make arrange-ments for Molly and Cameron.'

By now they had reached the kitchen, and the room came as another surprise to Izzy. This, too, had been completely refurbished, with magnifi-cent oak-fronted cabinets and deep shelving units bordered with decorative carving. As a cen-trepiece there was the huge range cooker that she remembered from long ago. To one side of the room were wine racks, filled with an assortment of bottles in colours ranging through green, red and brown to clear glass.

'I don't think I've seen *that* label before,' she murmured, looking more closely at the bottles. The designs were exotic, with beautiful Old English script overlaid on a watermark background of a castle in the glen, hinting at the richness of the wine within.

'They're our own label,' he told her. 'From what I'm fancifully calling the Glenmuir Winery. You should sit down at the table and try a glass or two.' He waved a hand towards the chair by an oak table to the side of the room. 'What do you fancy? We've a full-bodied elderberry, sweet and bursting with flavour, guaranteed to make you long for more, or there's oak leaf wine—dry, with a champagne flavour. We add raisins to that, and lemon juice to help bring it along. Maggie's favourite is the raspberry and bramble wine... light and fruity.'

She sent him a startled look. 'You're serious? Is this a new venture?'

He nodded. 'When I came over the other year I saw how many wild fruits we had growing on the estate and suggested that we might have a go at fermenting a batch. They turned out pretty well, so I'm looking into starting up a wine-making business. After all, we have acres of land here, just asking to be planted.'

He drew a bottle from the rack, placed it on the table, and then reached for a couple of wine-glasses from an overhead cupboard. 'Of course I'm not sure how people around here will respond to it. I doubt I'll be able to rely on them as customers. I'm facing a bit of resistance in trying to win them over to my side, one way or another. Even Maggie has a fairly sceptical view of my motives, but I think she feels she needs to look out for the children."

He was right about the locals. The talk in the village was all about the new Laird—an incomer who didn't belong. 'Maybe that's because you've been away for so long,' she murmured.

'After all, you weren't even educated here. Your father sent you away to school.'

'That's true. I dare say that's helped to provoke the feeling among the community that I'm an outsider.' He shrugged. 'Whatever the reason, I'm back now, and I have to do what I can to win them round.'

He smiled. 'Try this one,' he said, uncorking a bottle. 'See what you think. If you aren't completely bowled over, I'm an impostor from the Lakes.'

She sent him a fleeting glance. Had he read her mind? She shook the thought away. It was common knowledge that he would have to prove himself around here. Why was she worrying about the outcome?

He poured the rich ruby liquid into a glass and handed it to her. She sipped slowly, savouring the wine on her tongue before swallowing. A sweet, warm sensation enveloped her and she took another sip. She blinked, and then looked up at him.

'I think you must be the genuine article,' she murmured. 'This is delicious.'

'I'm glad you like it.' He poured more wine into the glass. 'Have some cheese with it, and crackers.' He laid out a selection of food and pushed a plate towards her, coming to join her at the table, taking a seat opposite.

'I don't know how you manage to pull it all in,' she said. 'You seem to have a lot of ideas and various projects on the go, and yet you're without an estate manager. How are you going to keep everything going?'

'Now, there you have me,' he said. 'Let's just say my plans are fairly fluid at the moment. A lot will depend on Alice and the children and how much support they need.'

She drank her wine, and tasted the cheese and crackers, and found after a while that she was oddly replete. A warm and comfortable feeling was enveloping her, with a general light-headed sensation that made her believe all was well with the world.

Ross excused himself to go and check on the children, but he was back just a short time later. 'Molly's still playing with her dolls' house, and Cameron's just launched a major offensive with his toy soldiers, so I think they'll be occupied for a while. Would you like to come and look at the grounds out back? I've been tidying up the kitchen garden whenever I've had the chance, and I've been thinking about a tree-planting scheme to break up the winds that blow across the north pasture in wintertime.'

She stood up and went with him to the kitchen door. 'Do the children know where we'll be?' she asked.

He nodded. 'I told them we might be looking out over the loch. They know to ring the bell that clangs outside if they have a problem of any kind.'

'That's a good idea.' She went with him to fetch her soft cord jacket from the cloakroom, shrugging into it as she walked out with him.

The cool air outside came as something of a surprise as she left the warmth of the kitchen behind. Her head swam a little with the after-effects of the wine, and Ross must have noticed because he put an arm around her, steadying her as he led her along the footpath towards the kitchen garden.

'I knew you'd appreciate the wine,' he said with a smile. 'It has quite a kick if you're not used to it.'

'You must have known that when you kept filling up my glass,' she accused. 'It's just as well that my on-call time finished an hour or so back, isn't it? At least I don't have to think about it again until morning.' She glanced at him, wondering how it was that the Buchanans were blessed with such strong features—the square jaw, the beautiful grey-blue eyes that looked at you and made you feel you were the only person that mattered in the whole world.

She tried to shake off that heady sensation. It was all in her mind, wasn't it? 'It looks as though you grow most of your own fruit and vegetables, here,' she murmured, gazing at long rows of planting.

'Well, we have a team of gardeners,' he said. 'It helps that they're all very good at what they do.'

They walked away from the kitchen gardens and around the side of the castle to a raised terrace, bordered by stone pediments and wrought iron balustrades, where they stood and looked out over the loch. The view was stunning. 'This is my favourite place,' Ross said softly.

'I can see why.' She gazed out at the gently rippling water, letting her glance move over green-clad hills and distant mountains shrouded in mist. 'It's so peaceful here. You can look out there and forget your troubles. It's so serene. I don't know how you can have stayed away.'

'You're right,' he said, wrapping his arm around her and drawing her close against the faint breeze. 'I often stand here and think perhaps things could have been different. It appears to be timeless here. I could have simply whiled away my days, looking out over the water and letting my thoughts drift.'

His hand stroked her arm and she laid her head on his shoulder, snuggling into the warmth of his body. Every part of her was content, loving this moment of deep quiet and calm. It seemed the most natural thing in the world to be standing here with him.

Except that it wasn't, of course. A cool wind blew across the loch, stirring the soft tendrils of her hair, and she looked up at him, blinking to bring her gaze back into sharp focus.

This was Ross Buchanan who was holding her close, shielding her from the cold. The same Ross Buchanan who had encouraged Alice to spend time in the castle and forget that her family was his sworn enemy. What was she thinking of, letting him ply her with wine and lead her out here to this beautiful place, a spot just begging for sweethearts to pledge eternal love? This was madness, being here with him.

She eased herself away from him, her head clearing rapidly in the cool breeze. 'I should go,' she said.

His glance moved over her. 'Are you sure?'

She nodded, not trusting herself to speak.

'All right. I'll gather up the children and drive you back to the cottage.'

He didn't seem at all put out by her need to leave. Had she imagined the intimacy of his warm embrace, the way he had held her so tenderly? He'd just been keeping her warm, steadying her because the drink had gone to her head, hadn't he? Anything else was pure supposition on her part.

CHAPTER FIVE

'BYE. Thanks for the lift home.' Izzy raised a hand, waving as Ross turned the car on the drive and headed back along the road.

She walked inside the cottage, her mind busy turning over the events of the last couple of hours. At least she was able to think more clearly now that the mist in her head had begun to dissolve. That fruit wine was sheer sin masquerading under a veil of innocence.

'Did I just see Ross Buchanan drop you off outside?' Her father confronted her as she stepped into the kitchen.

She sent him a startled look. 'Oh, hello. I didn't realise that you were here. Is your car at the front of the house?' Perhaps her faculties weren't as fully restored as she had hoped. 'I didn't see it out there.'

'That's because your mother dropped me off. She's gone over to the village shop, but she should be back soon. We just came by to bring you and Lorna a hotpot that she made. You know how she worries that you might not be feeding yourself properly.'

Across the other side of the kitchen, Lorna signalled that she had put the hotpot in the fridge. 'I'm going upstairs to get ready for nightshift at the hospital,' she said. 'I'll leave you two to chat for a while.'

Izzy nodded acknowledgement, then smiled at her father. 'I love Mum's hotpots. I'm sorry that I wasn't here when you arrived. Have you been here long?'

'Only about five minutes. Lorna said you'd nipped out for a while, but we weren't planning on stopping. We're on our way to go and visit your gran—but I just wanted to make sure that your roof wasn't leaking. I thought I'd take a look to see if my temporary patch was holding up.'

'Thanks for checking. It seems to be working all right… At least, we haven't had any damp patches on the ceiling so far. I think the roofer will be coming along to fix it in a day or so. Ross said he'd asked him to make it a priority.'

Her father's expression tightened. 'I notice that you didn't answer my question about him dropping you off. That was Ross I saw leaving, wasn't it? I went to look out of the window to see if it was you or your mother returning, and there was his fuel-guzzling monster outside.'

'He says it's the best vehicle to have on these roads in the winter. He has to drive over to Inverness quite regularly, so it's best for him to have a car that will be reliable and safe in snow and ice.'

Her father made a non-committal mumble at that, and she sent him a brief, considering look. 'Yes, I've been over to the castle and he brought me back.'

'So you've gone the way of Alice, have you? Spending your time up there? I thought you would have had more sense.'

'I took the children back to him,' she said, a wave of exasperation taking hold of her. 'They spent the afternoon with us, and I promised I would return them safely.' She gave a soft sigh. 'It's pointless to imagine that our paths will never cross. He's a doctor, and I have to work with him from time to time. We're not living in the Dark Ages, after all. It's something that you just have to get used to.'

'I'll never get used to it.' His voice was sharp. 'I don't see why he had to bring the children here at all. They could have stayed with Alice's sister.' He sent her a peevish glance. 'What does he know about bringing up youngsters, anyway?'

'Not very much, probably, which is why Alice is troubled.' She studied him. 'Look, I don't want to argue with you. I know how you feel. But I promised Alice I would look out for the children, and I aim to keep my promise—even if it means that I might rub shoulders with Ross from time to time. I don't see that it can do any harm, and he might not be as bad as you think.'

His eyes narrowed on her. 'I can see he's been working on you already. You'd do well to remember that the Buchanans never do anything by chance. There's always an ulterior motive lurking somewhere in the background. Like this business of the log cabin and the lodges he's building. It was all supposed to have been laid out crisp and clear, what he was doing and how far the building would extend, but now he's changing the format. I drove along the coastal road, where one of the lodges is under construction. It seemed to me that the building was wider than shown in the original drawings.'

'Will that matter?'

'Not necessarily, in itself, but what else might he decide to change? I don't trust him. Next thing he'll be adding garage blocks and new access roads, bringing more traffic along our way.'

'I'm sorry you feel like that about it.' Izzy's gaze was troubled. 'I hate to see you angry and upset. I understand how you feel, but surely you're reading too much into it. Perhaps we should all try to move on and put the past behind us?'

'You wouldn't feel that way if your livelihood depended on the goodwill of your neighbours. I had trouble with the old Laird, his father, and his constant attempts to stake a claim on my land with his tree planting and his new stone walls. Every now and again he would set up dams on the river to ruin the salmon fishing. He said it wasn't deliberate, but I never believed him.'

He scowled. 'His son hasn't done anything to remedy the problems along the course of the river in so much as they affect my being able to scratch a living, and now he's hatching a scheme to plant woodland that will block access to my cabins. We've always had a right of way to the old mill race, and now he thinks he can abandon it because he wants to set up a timber business. Without that footpath people will have to go the long way round to get to the holiday homes. He has a lot to answer for.' He glowered at her. 'It grieves me that my own daughter's getting involved with him.'

Izzy's mother arrived back from the shop in time to witness the tension between father and daughter. 'I knew it,' she said. 'As soon as I saw Ross's car heading up the hill away from here I knew I shouldn't have left you two together, even for five minutes.'

She gave Izzy a hug. 'Lorna put my hotpot in the fridge. Make sure you heat it through thoroughly…and I bought you a jar of coffee from Mary's shop. I noticed you were running short.'

'Thanks, Mum, you're an angel.'

'We'd best be going,' her father said, his tone abrupt. 'Your gran will be expecting us.'

Her mother went to the door. 'Perhaps we'll see you at the Christmas lights ceremony tomorrow evening?' she said. 'I'm running one of the stalls at a community centre…homemade crafts and pots of jam.'

Izzy embraced her parents and watched them drive away. It was upsetting to argue with her father. Would he ever come to see Ross Buchanan simply as a neighbour? Somehow she doubted it.

She tried not to think about the troublesome situation, and instead spent time getting on with various chores. Putting away freshly ironed laundry helped to lighten her mood.

The next day in the afternoon she was clearing away brambles from the garden when the phone rang. She hurried to answer it.

'The Mountain Rescue team has been called out.' Finn, a man in his late thirties who worked six days a week as the village postman, was also a member of the Mountain Rescue group, and now he said, 'We've had reports of a woman who has been injured on a crag by Beinn Dearg. Her companion used her mobile phone to call for help. She said she fell, and can't move without a lot of pain, so we have to get to her as soon as possible. I've already checked, and there's no way we'll be able to get a helicopter out to her, so it means we're in for a bit of a climb.'

'I'll get ready,' Izzy said.

'Good. I'll come and pick you up in five minutes.'

Finn was as good as his word, and within a very short time the whole team had assembled. 'We'll drive as close as we can to the hills before we need to start the climb,' Finn told them.

They started their trek from a forested area, heading for higher ground, keeping a tumbling stream to the left and below them. Izzy was startled to see that Ross had joined them somewhere along the route. 'You decided to give it a try, then?' she said.

'I did. I wanted to come out and see if it was something I'd like to do on a regular basis.' He looked out over the distant mountains. 'It's been quite a while since I did any climbing or hill walking. It's good to be able to help people, of course, and then there's always the aspect of keeping fit and enjoying the mountain trek.'

'What have you done with Molly and Cameron?'

'I left them with the local GP. They made friends with his children last week when I went over there to discuss a patient with him. In fact, he's going to be taking over the aftercare of the man who was injured by the waterfall.'

He walked beside her, and soon she was struggling to keep up with his long, rangy stride. Izzy studied him. 'You mean, the man with the pulmonary embolism? You know how he's doing, then?'

Ross nodded. 'His shoulder's still a bit sore, but they fixed the dislocation at the hospital and his ankle's in plaster. His breathing is much better, and he seems to be making a reasonably good recovery from his surgery, but of course his GP will have to keep an eye on him to make sure he doesn't suffer any more blood clots.'

'Yes, he will, but I'm glad that he's doing well over all.'

At one point they had to cross a stream, using flat rocks as stepping-stones, and Izzy hesitated for a moment, attempting to keep her balance. As she wavered, Ross placed a hand under her arm to steady her.

'Thanks,' she said, glancing up at him, her mouth making a rueful shape. 'I was just taking my time, that's all. The last thing I want is to spend the next few hours soaked to the skin.' She didn't want to notice his strength, or how capable he was, and how sure of foot he appeared to be, but it was true all the same. And as the heat from his hand at her elbow penetrated through the material of her jacket, it was more than enough to warm her through and through.

His eyes crinkled with amusement. 'No wine to blur your senses today,' he said. 'That's a shame. I quite liked it when you were soft and dreamy and wrapped up in my arms.'

They reached the other side of the stream and she threw him a quick glance. 'You were out of line yesterday,' she told him. He still was, if he thought he could sweet-talk her into getting close to him. She was more than wary on that score. 'You didn't tell me that your home brew packed such a punch. I thought—Fruit wine, lovely, no worries. If you do get a licence to sell your produce, at least you'll have to state the alcoholic content and people will know exactly what they're in for.'

He grinned. 'To be fair, I didn't realise it would hit you quite so hard. You probably hadn't eaten enough to soak it up.'

'Yes, well, I won't make that mistake again in a hurry.'

'That's a shame,' he said, affecting a down-turned mouth. 'I couldn't help thinking how great it was to see you looking so relaxed, and you were definitely happy to snuggle up and keep warm.'

She shot him a warning glance, and he laughed.

It took more than an hour of climbing over boulder slopes before they reached the point where the woman, who looked to be in her forties, was lying injured. She was resting on a narrow plateau at the foot of a ridge, and was in a bad way.

'Thank heaven you're here.' The woman's companion looked wretched. 'Sarah fell onto her side and hit the rock. I've been trying to keep her warm, but she's in an awful lot of pain.' She frowned. 'She's very shaky, and she seems to be not quite with me some of the time.'

'We'll take care of her,' Finn said. 'Come over and sit with the rest of our team and we'll give you a hot drink. You look as though you've had a pretty bad experience yourself. The doctors will look after your friend.'

Izzy knelt down beside the woman. 'Hello, there. Sarah, is it?'

Sarah struggled to focus, but then she slowly, almost imperceptibly nodded.

Izzy said quietly, 'I'm Dr McKinnon, and here with me is Dr Buchanan. We'll have a look at you and try to make you more comfortable, and then the Mountain Rescue team will take you back down the slopes and on to hospital as quickly as possible. Can you tell me where-abouts you're hurting?'

Sarah vaguely indicated the region of her hip. Her face was pale, and etched with pain, and when Izzy carefully examined her she could see that on her injured side the leg was shorter than the other one, with the toes pointing out.

She glanced at Ross. 'I think she has a pelvic fracture,' she said softly.

He nodded. 'I agree with you.' He checked the woman's pulse and respiration as Izzy began to open up her medical bag. 'Her heart-rate is very fast, and so is her breathing,' he said in a low voice. 'I suspect she's going into shock because of internal bleeding.'

That was bad news. Untreated shock meant that the patient's condition could deteriorate very rapidly. 'Okay. We'll give her oxygen and put in an intravenous line so that we can give her fluids to replace the blood loss.' She spoke gently to her patient. 'Sarah, I believe you have a broken bone in your pelvis. I'm going to give you an injection for the pain. It should make you feel much more comfortable.'

As soon as they had completed those procedures, and Sarah's pain had retreated, Izzy worked with Ross to immobilise the injury by means of a splint. He was calm and efficient, capable in everything he did, and above all he was caring and considerate towards the woman.

Izzy turned to the other members of the rescue team. 'We need to lift her onto the stretcher,' she said, 'keeping her as still as possible.'

'No problem,' Finn said. 'Between us we can do that.'

They all worked together to transfer Sarah to the stretcher, covering her with a blanket and fastening the straps securely to prevent her from slipping and coming to any more harm. After that it was a question of carrying her back down the slope.

'I've called the emergency services and asked them to have an ambulance waiting for us,' Izzy said.

Two members of the team came forward to

take hold of the stretcher, while Finn stayed with the woman's friend, keeping her company as they started back down the slope. Izzy took a moment to gaze around, looking down across the valley to the distant loch. Mist was rolling in over the mountains and the smooth silver surface of the water, signifying the close of the afternoon and a cooling temperature.

'I was really glad of your help back there,' she told Ross. 'It meant that we could treat her much more quickly and get her on her way. Time is the enemy here, isn't it?'

'It is when it's a bad injury like that one. The sooner we get her to hospital the better.'

They moved as swiftly as possible, all of them anxious to reach safe ground before nightfall. Other members of the team took over the stretcher-bearing, to give the first two a rest. Eventually they reached the forest once more, and Izzy paused to check on the status of her patient. 'It's all right, we can keep moving,' she told the rest of the team. 'She seems to be holding up well enough.'

When they finally reached the place where they had parked the rescue team's van, Izzy watched over the transfer of her patient to the ambulance and helped Sarah's friend to settle in beside her while Ross went to speak to the paramedics.

Satisfied that Sarah was comfortable, Izzy climbed down from the vehicle. Finn came to meet her. 'A job well done, I think. We've a good group of people here, and with you and Ross on call the people around here can rest easy.'

'Do you think he'll decide to join the Mountain Rescue team?' she asked. 'I gather this was something of a trial run for him.'

'I hope he will. I remember some years ago he used to do all sorts of outdoor activities—hill-walking, climbing, abseiling, to name just a few. Of course then he went off to do his medical training, and there was all that business with Alice.' Finn spoke in a low voice. 'It was a bad time all round when his brother stole her away from him. There was a breakdown of trust, if you like…not that they had ever been one hundred percent on brotherly love. Robert loved the estate, but Ross was the elder brother, and Robert tended to brood. I imagine that's why he left in the end. Though it was a bad day when he took Alice with him.'

Izzy mulled that over. How must Ross have felt when his brother betrayed his trust? Things had always been difficult between them, but that must have hurt badly. Had they still been arguing years later, as her mother had said, when the accident happened? And did that mean that Ross would now be wondering if he might get another chance with Alice? Was that the true reason he had come home? Did he want to be close to Alice?

A bleak wave of despondency washed over her—a feeling she couldn't explain, even to herself. She loved Alice as a sister, but her feelings for Ross went far deeper than that and were more complex, fraught with problems and complications.

She pushed those thoughts aside as Ross came to join them after he'd finished speaking with the paramedics. Within moments the ambulance had set off on its journey to Inverness.

'I hope she'll be all right,' Izzy said. 'We moved as quickly as we could, but these situations are difficult. The outcome isn't always what you would hope for.'

'Her age might work in her favour,' Ross said. 'She was fit and healthy before this, so we just have to keep our fingers crossed that all will go well for her. At least they're on alert at the hospital.'

Finn nodded. 'We can be on our way home now, anyway. Shall I be taking you back with me, Izzy?'

'It's out of your way, isn't it, Finn?' Ross said. 'I can take Izzy home.' He shot her a quick look. 'If that's all right with you? I have to pick up the children from Tom Slater's house on the way.'

'That's fine.' They started to walk towards the cars. 'I imagine we'll all be meeting up at the Christmas lights ceremony fairly soon, anyway. Although my offer still stands… I can take the children with me, if you would sooner opt out?'

Ross shook his head. 'I don't think that's an option—even though a majority of the villagers might prefer it if I stay away.'

Finn acknowledged that with a rueful smile.

'I'll see you both later,' he said. 'Thanks for your help today.'

Izzy was still thinking about Ross's comment. It was sad that people couldn't see beyond ancient feuds. She said goodbye to Finn and the other members of the group, and then went to stand by Ross's car.

'I don't imagine for one minute that Molly and Cameron will hear of me staying at home,' Ross said as he started the engine. 'They're hoping that I'll buy all sorts of things…Christmas decorations, for a start. Apparently those I dragged down from the attic are way too ordinary, and something far more spectacular is called for—or at least that's what they told Alice this morning.'

'Of course—you went to see her, didn't you? How is she?' Oddly, Izzy felt warmth seep all around her as she settled more comfortably in her seat. A puzzled look came over her face, and she caught Ross's quick glance.

His mouth curved. 'The seats are heated,' he said. 'It was cold up there on Beinn Dearg, so I thought you might appreciate the warmth.'

She nodded. 'Oh, I do. Just as I appreciated the hot coffee that Finn offered me. They're very well prepared for these trips, aren't they?'

'True.' He concentrated on the road as he came to a junction, and then he said lightly, 'I thought Alice was looking a little better today. It always cheers her up to see the children, and they seem to encourage her to keep on with the physiotherapy. She's beginning to walk around with help from the physios, and that's a good sign.'

'Yes, it is.' Izzy was thoughtful for a while after that. It wasn't lost on her that Alice's cheeks always burned a little brighter whenever Ross was around. He had helped her through so much these last few months, and now he was taking care of her children. That was bound to make her appreciative of him.

Ross dropped her off at the cottage a short time later, after the children had bombarded her with talk of their exploits at the GP's house. They were now very friendly with the doctor's children, it seemed, and they were looking forward to meeting up with them later on at the lights ceremony.

Izzy hurried to get ready for the evening ahead. 'I'm off now,' Lorna told her. 'But I'll see you later in the community hall.'

Izzy grabbed a bite to eat, and then went to change into a clean pair of jeans and a warm top. She ran a brush through her long hair, and added a touch of lipstick to her mouth.

A knock at the door startled her, but then she heard childish voices, and when she went to find out who was there she saw Ross with Molly and Cameron.

'We came to give you a lift,' he said. 'I wondered if you might need a bit of cosseting after today's efforts.'

'What a wonderful thought…though you worked just as hard as I did. That was some trek, there and back, wasn't it?' She smiled at the gathering on her doorstep, noting how Molly and Cameron were turning towards the car. 'I can see you're all eager to be off, so I'll fetch my bag and we're all set.'

When she came back to them, Ross slid an arm around her waist, leading her out to his vehicle and gently assisting her into the passenger seat. She tried not to read anything into that. He was just being himself. He would have done the same for Lorna or anyone else who happened to be female, probably. What was it Lorna had said? He had loads of charisma and easy charm, and without even trying he knew just how to set a woman's heart racing.

'Hop in, you two,' he said to the children. 'Buckle up.'

In the village, a crowd had congregated around the huge tree on the common, and after the local dignitary had made his speech and led the countdown for the lights to be switched on they all sang carols, their breath misting on the cold air.

Perhaps that cold had seeped into Cameron, because he started to cough. Izzy drew him close to her, wrapping an arm around him and keeping him warm. 'Are you all right?' she asked him quietly.

He nodded. 'Can we go round the fair rides, now?' he asked. 'I want to drive the train engine.'

'And I want to go on the horses that go up and down,' Molly said. She was tugging at Ross's trousers, pulling him in the direction of the small amusements section, where roundabouts and candyfloss stalls had been set out in a small side road by the tree-clad embankment.

'Okay, okay—I'm coming.' He glanced at Izzy, taking her by the hand, and they both followed the children, who were running off in the direction of the rides.

'Why is it that children are never still?' Ross said some half an hour later, as they came out of the fish and chip shop and walked back towards the community hall, biting into hot chips from overflowing cones.

Izzy fanned her mouth to take away the heat of the potato. 'Because there's always something new to be explored,' she said. 'I expect you were just the same when you were that age.'

He laughed. 'I suppose I was.' They stood and finished off their salt-and-vinegar-slathered chips at the side of a building, basking in the golden pool of light from the nearby shop.

Cameron handed Izzy his empty carton. 'I've finished,' he said. 'Can we go into the community hall now?'

'All right.' Izzy dropped all the cartons into a wastebin and wiped her hands on a tissue.

They walked into the crowded hall, and Ross took Molly to find Christmas decorations while Izzy went to see how her mother was getting on with the crafts stall.

'Everything looks lovely,' Izzy told her. 'I don't suppose you'll be left with much at the end of the evening.'

'Good. It's all for the children's charity,' her mother said. 'I want everything to go.'

'I like those boxes,' Cameron said, pointing to a small trinket box decorated with quilled scrolls and flower motifs. 'Mum would love one of those for her Christmas present.' He counted out coins from his pocket and handed them over to Izzy's mother, waiting patiently while she wrapped it up.

'I'm sure she'll be over the moon with it,' Izzy's mother said. 'It's very pretty, isn't it?'

Cameron nodded, caught out by another bout of coughing. Izzy took his purchase and watched him carefully. 'I think you might be starting a cold,' she said. She felt his forehead with the back of her hand. 'You've a bit of a temperature, too. Maybe we ought to get you home soon.'

'I don't want to go home yet.' He coughed again.

'I can't think why that boy's out and about, with a cough like that,' Izzy's father said, coming over to them from a nearby stall. 'What's Ross thinking of, bringing him here? Those children could just as easily have stayed with their aunt down in the Lake District, where they had their friends and went to school.'

Izzy pressed her lips together, biting back a reply as she saw Ross coming towards them. From his taut expression, it was clear he had heard what her father had said, and her heart sank with the knowledge that those few curt words might bring a fraught end to what had been a lovely evening.

'Are you all right, Cameron?' Ross asked.

The boy nodded. 'I want to look at the toy stall,' he said.

'Okay. Take Molly with you. I'll be there in a minute.' Ross watched the children go, and then turned to acknowledge Izzy's mother. 'You have some beautiful items here, Morag,' he said. 'I'll take one of the flower pictures for Alice. I know she likes those.' He handed over the money and looked towards Izzy's father. 'Cameron will be fine,' he said. 'He has a cold, that's all. He's a sturdy boy.'

'Let's hope so.' Her father's gaze narrowed on him. 'I still think it's strange, uprooting them from where they were happy.'

Ross looked at him steadily. 'This is their heritage,' he said. 'They have every right to be here and know the place where their father was born. I see no reason to apologise for that.'

He accepted the package from Izzy's mother and said, 'Excuse me. I must go and find the children.'

Izzy's gaze followed him, her heart squeezing a little. Had he really brought them here to know the ancient heritage that went through generation after generation? He was a proud man, steadfast in his beliefs, and she respected him for that— just as she understood why her father responded to him in his edgy, confrontational manner. She loved her father, and it saddened her to see them at loggerheads like this. All Ross had to do was unbend a little and try to meet him half way. Why could he not do that?

CHAPTER SIX

'HAVE you heard the latest?' Lorna broke the crust of her steak pie with the side of her fork and speared the tender meat.

'No, but I'm sure you're about to tell me.' Izzy tasted the crunchy roast potato on her plate, and then followed it up with a forkful of carrots. It was early evening and they were sitting in the lounge bar of the Shore Inn, close by the large fireplace where hot coals burned in the grate.

'Ross has brought a film crew to the castle,' Lorna said. 'They're all talking about it at the bar. Greg was just telling me he was held up on the road into the village the other day because of their truck with all the equipment. He wasn't best pleased. He said it made him late for work.'

'A film crew?' Izzy echoed. 'What kind of film are they making? Do we know?'

Lorna shrugged. 'I've no idea—but something swashbuckling, I bet. Apparently there was a horsebox in the line of traffic that kept Greg waiting, so I expect there'll be scenes of riders dashing across the bridge up to the castle. Sounds exciting, doesn't it?'

'It certainly does.' Izzy's eyes sparkled. 'This is the first time we've had anything like that happening around here. I wonder what the rest of the villagers will think about it?'

'The landlord's hoping they'll be here for quite a while,' Lorna said, waving her fork lightly in the air before scooping up a mouthful of mashed potato. 'He's looking forward to having more customers, and Mary at the shop is apparently checking her stock for things they might want—like souvenirs to take home, postcards and so on.'

Greg came to join them at their table. 'They're all full of it back there,' he said, sitting down and taking a long swig from his glass. 'I'd say it's about half and half, those in favour and those against.' He put the glass down. 'I suppose the people who keep the hotel are quite pleased, too. With all those film folk needing a place to stay, trade will be looking up.'

'I heard some of the others say that it's an odd time to be filming,' Lorna commented, 'with the threat of snow in the air. But I suppose if they're filming inside the castle that won't really matter. They could do all the outside shots first. That's the thing with filming, isn't it—you do things out of sequence?'

'I suppose that's true,' Greg answered, staring into the fire. 'Not that I get much chance to watch films these days, let alone see them being made. After working at the A&E unit all day, and travelling to Inverness two or three times a week, I'm too shattered to take much notice of anything else going on.'

He sent a glance in Izzy's direction. 'Your Alice is looking much better of late, by the way. Apparently the children have an Advent calendar to help them to count down to Christmas, but they seem to think it's also like counting off the days until she'll come home. Ross has had to explain to them that it's a bit more complicated than that.'

Izzy smiled at him. 'It's comforting to know that you see Alice on a regular basis. I've been trying to get over there as often as I can, but it isn't always easy with work getting in the way. Mostly I've been going over of an evening.'

A strange silence fell in the usually noisy lounge of the inn, and a faint breeze wafted into the room as someone opened the outer door. Izzy looked around to see why the chatter had suddenly come to a stop, and saw Ross's tall figure in the doorway.

He looked around and nodded to the various people sitting at tables or standing by the bar. The landlord gave him a cheery welcome, but Izzy could see that others were hesitant.

'What will you have?' the landlord said.

'A half of lager and a ploughman's, please.'

'Coming up. Are you on your way home, or are you planning on staying a while?' He started to pour out the lager, and then pushed a platter of baguette, cheese and salad towards Ross. 'We're all keen to know what's going on up at the castle with all your visitors. Is Maggie catering for them all? I'm not sure how that would go down with her.'

Ross shook his head. 'Maggie has enough to do already. When she's not seeing to the meals and doing the housework she's looking after Molly and Cameron for me. The people at the hotel are sending out a selection of hot food for the film crew by van every morning, but I dare say you could get in on the act if you wanted. There's bound to be someone who wants something other than what's provided.'

'I might look into that. So, they're all staying at the hotel, are they? No hope of any leading ladies being entertained up at the castle after hours, then?' the landlord teased.

'Oh, I wouldn't go as far as to say that,' Ross said with a smile. 'They've only been here for a couple of days, but I'm getting quite used to having them around.'

'It's all right for some.' A disgruntled male voice

sounded across the room. 'Some people were born with the proverbial silver spoon in the mouth.'

'Maybe it's lucky you weren't, then,' Ross came back, quick as a flash. 'With a mouth like that you might easily have choked.' A faint hum of laughter went around the room.

'With all this money rolling in from the filming, you'll be able to put the rents down hereabouts, then?' someone else said. Izzy recognised a man who worked as a carpet fitter in the nearby town.

'I seem to remember a hefty bill for the new carpets I just had laid down at the castle. Will you be charging everyone less for your services in the future?' Ross raised a dark brow. 'When that day comes, I might consider it.'

The man made a face, and after that the general conversation resumed. Ross looked around and came over to Izzy's table.

'Hello, there,' he said. 'Might I join you?'

'Of course.' Izzy waved a hand towards the empty seat next to Greg. She and Lorna had both finished eating, and they pushed their plates to one side. 'We were just talking about the film crew descending on the village. How did that come about?'

'They approached me some time ago and I agreed that they could do a shoot. I decided the fee would come in handy for the tree-planting. It's only now that they've managed to fix their schedule.'

'Are we talking documentary or entertainment?' Greg asked. 'And how about top actors and actresses? I think the girls here are hoping for swashbuckling heroes and lots of derring-do.'

Ross nodded. 'That's not too far off. A couple of top names, too. But I don't think they'll be around for long—maybe a week or two at most. They're only shooting a few scenes here. The rest will be done at studios.'

'I hope I'm to have an invitation to come and see them in action,' Lorna said, looking brazenly optimistic. 'I could always make myself useful—providing cups of tea and so on.'

'By all means,' Ross agreed with a smile. 'Consider yourself invited...you, too, Izzy—

and Greg. I'll be at home mid-week in the after-
noons. I'm not sure, but maybe they'll be
looking for extras.'

'Whoo-hoo.' Lorna chuckled. 'Hollywood,
here I come.'

'Now, see—she's getting carried away,' Izzy
said, her mouth curving. She sent Ross a dispar-
aging glance. 'Now look what you've done.'

'It isn't fair,' he said, his jaw dropping as he
looked from one to the other. 'I get the blame for
everything around here.'

'Always have done, always will,' Greg
murmured, and they all laughed.

They talked for some time about the film crew,
and their work at the hospital, and the air ambulance and mutual friends.

'I must go,' Izzy said after a while. 'It's getting
late, and I have to sort out a few things before
morning. I'm on call with the ambulance team
from the early hours, so I need to be organised
and ready.' She glanced at Lorna. 'Are you
staying for a while?'

Lorna nodded. 'I have a day off tomorrow…

several hours all to myself…so I plan to take it easy. I expect Greg will give me a lift home— won't you, Greg?'

'Of course.'

Izzy stood up to take her leave of them, and Ross said, 'I'll walk you to your car. I need to go home and relieve the babysitter.'

They left the pub together, and Izzy paused for a moment by her car. 'I think it's good that you came to mix with the locals for a while,' she said softly. 'It's the only way that you're going to break down the barriers.'

'Do you think I need to do that?' he asked.

'If you want to be accepted around here, yes, I do,' she said. 'You might think that you can turn your back on criticism, but I don't think that will do you any good in the long run.' For some reason she cared deeply about how he fitted in here. She wanted him to be accepted, to be part of the fabric of her home village.

'I don't see why I should have to explain myself to anyone,' he said, coming to stand beside her. 'I grew up with half these people.

They should know who I am and what I believe in. If they can't accept me for who I am, then that's their problem.'

'So you don't think that their worries about rents are of any consequence? Or that any unsettled feelings they might have about leasing land they feel is already rightfully theirs has anything to do with you?'

'Why do you care about what they think of me, either way?' He said it softly, but it was a challenge all the same.

'You're right. Why should I?' Perhaps he hadn't meant it in a harsh manner, but she braced herself, standing up very straight, unwilling to show any sign of weakness. Caring about someone who was heading helter-skelter into a quagmire was always going to be a difficult business. It led to all sorts of doubts and concerns, and it undermined confidence. But the fact was she did care, very deeply, about Ross Buchanan. Try as she might to tell herself that his problems were not hers, the thought had a hollow ring. How was it that he had managed to work his way into her affections?

He reached out a hand and lightly stroked the soft silk of her hair. Heat rose in her as his fingers left behind a trail of fire. 'Much as I appreciate your concern, you don't need to worry about me,' he said. 'I promise you I can take care of myself.'

'I know that.' That was the problem, wasn't it? He was proud, some might say arrogant, but his attitude was all part and parcel of the way people around here felt about him. 'It's just that a lot of these problems are not actually truly yours. They're hand-me-downs from your father, and from the fallout from your brother leaving. No matter what people say, I think you have an affinity with this place. It's in your soul. It's part of you.'

'So you don't see me as an outsider? I know that's how others think of me.'

'I don't.' She was all too conscious of his fingers threading through her hair, of the way his thumb lightly trailed along the line of her jaw. That faint touch was enough to send her whole body into meltdown. Why was he being so gentle with her? Caressing her as though she mattered to him? Was he simply flirting with her because it came to him as naturally as breathing air?

Her parents' warnings came back to her a hundredfold. She should stay away from him. He was trouble—a man at odds with himself and with the world in general.

'You didn't come back here after you qualified as a doctor—I think people expected that you would do that, but you stayed away. Perhaps while your brother was alive you felt you couldn't take the reins. I don't know. I don't know what was going through your mind. But I don't believe that you had no interest in coming back.'

Perhaps the simple truth was that he'd wanted to be where Alice was? Why else had he followed them, leaving his home village shortly after his brother?

'There was nothing complicated going on,' he said. 'I worked hard to become a doctor, and I enjoy the work I do. With no family to provide for, there was no need for me to come back and become Laird.' He let his hand fall to his side. 'Whatever the crofters say, the rents are fair. I've looked into it, and the charges are reasonable. Perhaps the real problem is that they don't want to be tenants at all. They want ownership, and that is quite a different thing. It's a huge responsibility and one not to be taken lightly—as I've discovered.'

She sent him a thoughtful glance. 'And that's the reason why you've allowed a film crew to invade your family home, is it? You have the responsibility of making it all work. It's the reason you're planting trees and planning to start your own winery. Perhaps you're not thinking about going away after all? And if that's the case you really need to work on getting along with the people around you.'

'What a great adviser you are,' he said, his tone lightly mocking. 'Perhaps I should persuade you to come and be my personal assistant—to guide me through the shark-infested waters.'

She lifted her brows. 'Is that another action plan—to market the castle as having a loch where sea monsters lurk?'

He made a soft chuckle. 'I can see you're a

force to be reckoned with, Izzy. You don't deal in romantic fantasy, do you? Everything is cut and dried, and you can see it all so very clearly. There are no blurred lines, no greying of images or taking the option of letting things ride to see how they work out. You're certainly your father's daughter, aren't you? You see everything with a clinical eye.'

He moved in closer to her. 'Perhaps I should work on that and try to win you round to my point of view. I could show you how to be more laid-back, more lackadaisical about what people think. Perhaps I could persuade you to think of me more fondly.'

The trouble was he could probably do it, too. She was already thinking of him far more than was good for her. She eased herself away from the car, away from his circle of power. 'I must go,' she said. 'You'll do as you please—as always. I'm just sorry that you might be wasting a golden opportunity to turn this community around.'

His mouth curved in amusement. 'It isn't this community that I'm concerned about,' he murmured. 'I'm much more interested in a sweet-natured girl with chestnut coloured hair and a figure straight out of paradise. I've always wanted you, Izzy. You've always been the girl for me.'

'No—don't say that. I don't believe it. Not for a minute. Alice was the one you wanted, the one you flirted with and kept close by. It was always Alice.' How could he even say otherwise? His words stung her far more deeply than she might have expected. Was he playing with her? Teasing her? It had always been Alice that he loved. Everyone knew that.

He shook his head. 'You're wrong, Izzy. It wasn't like that.'

'I can't talk to you,' she said, pulling open the door of her car and sliding into the driver's seat. He was treating her as a would-be conquest—someone to be won over to his side. 'You're impossible.'

She started up the engine and backed out of her parking slot. Her exit was more a desperate escape than a strategically planned retreat. The last she saw of him, he was standing by the fence, watching her drive away, and she felt a sudden qualm of loss, her emotions pricking her, chiding her for not ignoring her inner warning system and staying a while longer.

Perhaps it was fortunate that her work kept her from dwelling too closely on thoughts of Ross and how he made her feel.

The next day, as she was progressing from one callout to the next, it began to snow. It started with a light dusting of flakes at around lunch-time, and by the middle of the afternoon it was coming down like a thick curtain, settling on the fields and the hedgerows, coating everything with a layer of frosty peaks.

At any other time it would have been a wondrous sight. Looking out over the snow-capped mountains and gazing in wonder at the white-spangled branches of the pine trees would have been a vision to melt the stoniest heart. Now, though, as Izzy drove along a country lane to her next call, it only made her conscious of how difficult it was going to be to return home along these icy, snow-clogged roads.

She reached her destination—an isolated farm-house, set back among trees and bordered by a huddle of barns and outbuildings.

A harassed-looking man, with hair that appeared as though he had been raking his hands through it for the last hour or so, greeted her at the door of the house.

'Are you the doctor? I was so afraid you wouldn't get here,' he said. 'The midwife is stuck in snow, and they say the ambulance will be some half an hour or more yet. My wife, Jenny, is having the baby. It's not due for another week, but she's definitely in labour. I don't know what to do.'

'Perhaps you should take me to her,' Izzy murmured, 'and I'll see how far she is along.'

'I will—of course. Here, let me take one of your bags.'

'Thanks.' She handed him the one with the oxygen equipment, and he weighed it in his hand briefly.

'It feels as though you must have everything you need in here,' he said. 'It's pretty heavy.'

'I have most of the things I might need in the car,' she told him. 'We come supplied for emergencies.'

He led the way up the stairs to the main bedroom, where his wife, a woman of around thirty years old, was lying on the bed, pale-faced and covered in beads of sweat.

A look of relief came into her eyes as Izzy walked into the room.

'Hello, Jenny,' Izzy said, going over to greet her and check her condition. 'Let's see if we can make you more comfortable, shall we? How often are the contractions coming?'

'Every…couple…of minutes,' Jenny answered, pain contorting her features. She looked as though she was about to pass out.

Izzy checked her blood pressure and listened to her heart. Then she checked the foetus's heart-beat, listening carefully for any sign that it might be in distress.

'Your blood pressure is very low, Jenny,' she said. 'I'm going to turn you over on to your left side. That should help to relieve the pressure and make you feel a little better.'

Turning to Jenny's husband, Izzy said, 'We're going to need to clean towels and a crib for the baby. Do you have one? Otherwise, something like a laundry basket will do.'

'I…um…yes. I can see to that.' He looked as though he was glad to be given something practical to do.

In the meantime, it was clear to Izzy that the baby's arrival was imminent. She gave Jenny pain relief through a mask held over her nose and mouth. As another contraction started, Izzy examined Jenny once more.

'I can see the baby's head,' she said. 'Try to push with each contraction. That's it.'

The contraction faded, and Jenny sank back against her pillows.

The woman's husband came back into the room. 'I didn't know how many towels you might need,' he said, 'so I brought them all.' He laid them down on the end of the bed and then swivelled around, looking bemused, as though he wasn't sure what to do next.

Izzy looked at him. 'The crib?' she said.

'Oh, yes. I'll go and get it.' He hesitated, his expression blank, and then stared at his wife as though she might provide the answer.

Jenny had other things on her mind. Another contraction overwhelmed her, and she concentrated on pushing as hard as she could.

'It's coming,' Izzy said. 'You're doing really well.'

As the head appeared, Izzy worked quickly to clear secretions from the baby's nose and mouth. 'That's great, Jenny. Rest now. Wait for the next contraction.'

Her husband stood at the side of the bed, overwhelmed and uncertain.

'James, weren't you going to look for something?' Jenny reminded him wearily.

'Was I?'

'The crib?' she suggested.

'Oh, yes.' He looked confused.

'Try the baby's room,' Jenny murmured in a resigned tone.

'Of course.' He gave a sigh of relief. 'Yes, of course—that's where it is.'

Izzy began to smile, but Jenny merely looked exasperated and lay back, worn out by her exertions. 'Men,' she muttered.

More contractions followed, and within minutes the baby was born. Izzy said softly, 'It's a little boy. You have a beautiful boy, Jenny.' She wrapped the infant in a clean towel, drying it as quickly as she could. Then she gently rubbed the baby's back until he gave a soft cry.

Izzy clamped the umbilical cord in two places, and then cut between the clamps. As soon as she had checked that all was well, she wrapped the baby snugly once more and handed him to his mother.

It was a joyous, wonderful moment for the parents, but it was equally exhilarating for Izzy. To be privileged enough to help a baby into the world was always a breathtaking experience, one that she cherished.

Would she one day have a child of her own? It was something she almost dared not think about—because she had a strong feeling that the one man she would even remotely consider for its father was perhaps the one man she could not have.

A few minutes later the afterbirth was delivered, and Izzy checked that the mother was comfortable and that her blood pressure and respiration were normal.

'What's the betting that the midwife and the ambulance will both arrive now that my baby is safely here?' Jenny said. She stroked her baby's cheek and nestled against James, who had come to sit beside her.

Sure enough the doorbell rang a few minutes later, and Izzy glanced out of the window to see who was there. 'It looks as though your midwife *has* arrived,' Izzy said. 'I'll go and let her in. I expect she'll want to stay with you for a while, to make sure that all is well.'

Izzy handed her patient over to the midwife, and then tidied up all her equipment and said goodbye.

James went with her to the door. 'I'll put your bags in the car for you,' he said. 'I can't thank you enough for all that you've done. I've no idea how I would have coped if you hadn't turned up.'

'I'm sure you would have managed some-how,' Izzy said.

She started back along the road, heading for home. Her stint on call had finished now, and she was looking forward to getting back to the cottage and home comforts.

The road, though, was treacherous. She drove carefully, taking her time, and after twenty minutes or so of travelling she began to wonder when the snowplough would reach this area. There was ice everywhere and now darkness was falling, bringing an eerie quality to the surrounding area.

She was still some half an hour away from home, and there were no other cars on this stretch of country road. As she negotiated a bend, her car skidded, not responding to her attempts to straighten up, and she went headlong into a snowdrift. The engine stalled and spluttered, and then there was silence.

Izzy waited for a moment or two and then tried to start the engine once again. Nothing happened.

She sat for some time, wondering what she ought to do next, and after a while took a torch out of the glove compartment and climbed out of the car to see what the problem might be.

The car had come to rest at an angle, on the verge by an ancient tree, and just a few inches away the ground sloped towards a ditch. Judging by the angle of the car, and the way it was embedded deep in snow, she doubted she would be able to push it free. Even so, she gave it a go.

Nothing doing. She sat back in the car and tried the radio. It cut out after a few seconds. After a few more attempts she gave up trying, and used her phone to call the garage.

After that, she settled down to wait. The garage was some half an hour distant from here, and they were busy with an unprecedented amount of calls. She had no idea how long it would be before she was rescued.

She was shivering a little, and her teeth had begun to chatter, when she eventually heard the sound of a vehicle approaching. Surely this must be the garage rescue service? Would the driver see her in the darkness? Quickly, she flashed the car lights to draw the driver's attention.

It wasn't the rescue service that had come to her aid, though. It was Ross.

'Good grief, Izzy…of all the times to choose to go and drive yourself into a ditch.' He pulled open her car door and reached for her, pulling her into his arms. 'You're freezing,' he said. 'Come on into my car and let's get you warmed up.' He looked at her. 'I know you like the heated seats, but you didn't have to go this far to get yourself a ride.'

She bunched her cold fingers into a fist and feebly thumped him on the arm. 'I'm really not in the mood for jokes,' she said.

CHAPTER SEVEN

THE interior of Ross's car was comfortingly warm and inviting. Izzy huddled in the passenger seat while Ross enveloped her in a blanket and supplied her with hot coffee from a vacuum flask. She wrapped her fingers around the cup and revelled in the heat it provided.

'Is that better?' he asked, coming to sit beside her.

'Much better,' she said. 'I'm beginning to feel a little more human now. I'm sorry if I snapped at you.'

'Snapping is allowed when you're suffering from near hypothermia,' he murmured.

She made a rueful smile. 'It seemed like an eternity, sitting in that freezing car, waiting. I'd no idea how long it was going to be before anyone turned up. The garage boss told me they were overrun with callouts. It seems a lot of people have broken down or got stuck in the snow.' She frowned. 'How is it that *you're* here, anyway? I was expecting a mechanic to come along and sort out my problem eventually. I was hoping that maybe he would be able to get me back on the road.'

He nodded. 'That will still happen. They're going to send out a rescue vehicle. As it happens, I was at the garage when your call came through…my car was in for a service and I'd just arrived to pick it up. As you say, they were inundated with calls, and worried that they might not be able to get out to you anytime soon, so I offered to come and find you.'

'Oh, I see.' She sent him a grateful glance. 'Well, thank you for that.' She sipped her hot coffee, more to steady her nerves than anything else. 'It was a bit of a shock, going off the road that way, and then with it being dark and isolated it was all a bit creepy. I didn't realise trees and branches could make such malevolent shapes against the skyline. I guess my imagination was working overtime. I was really relieved when you came along.'

'I can imagine it must have been a scary experience for you,' Ross acknowledged. 'Everything looks grimmer in the dark, doesn't it?' He frowned. 'Unfortunately, I don't think there's anything we can do to get you back on the road this evening, though. I've had a look around, and there seems to be some oil spillage on the ground, so something has probably been damaged underneath the car. I've transferred most of your equipment to this vehicle, so there shouldn't be any worries on that score.'

'I suppose not. And at least I'll be able to use my own car to go into work tomorrow. I'm actually only on duty for the morning. At least I'm not meant to be out on call, and hopefully whatever's wrong with the fast response vehicle can be repaired in a fairly short time.' She fell silent, finishing off her hot drink, and then returned the cup to him. Oddly, her hand was shaking, and as she turned to face him she became aware of a dull pain in her shoulder, causing her to wince.

Perhaps she was more traumatised by her ordeal than she had realised. It was one thing to be cold and cut off from civilisation, but it was quite another to have narrowly missed being catapulted into a ditch.

He wrapped his arms around her. 'It's all right, you're safe now.' He looked at her, his expression concerned. 'Are you hurt in any way? Maybe I should take a look at you?'

'No, I'm okay,' she said hurriedly. There was no way she wanted him examining her. 'I think the seat belt must have bruised me a little because I shot forward with some force. I'm sure there's nothing broken or damaged too much— it's just a bit of muscular pain.'

'Poor you.' He didn't push the issue, but instead soothingly stroked her cheek and gently held her, coaxing her to lean into the hollow of his shoulder, cradling her head against him with his hand.

That tenderness was her undoing. She snuggled against him, loving the strength and warmth of his long body, mesmerised by the way he was lightly caressing her as though she was the most precious thing in the world to him. It made her feel safe and secure. As if everything was going to be fine now that he was here.

'Are you feeling a little warmer now?'

She nodded. 'I am—thank you. It was thoughtful of you to bring along a hot drink. You must have guessed I would need it.'

'I believe in being prepared.' He studied her features in the car's interior light. 'There's a little more colour in your cheeks now, at any rate.'

She lifted her face to him. 'I didn't expect to feel this way. I always thought I would cope fairly well in a crisis…I didn't imagine that I would crumble at the first post.'

He smiled into her eyes. 'I don't see too much crumbling—just a young woman recovering from a frightening experience. Thank heaven for mobile phones.'

She laughed, her mouth softening as she drank in his smoky grey-blue gaze. 'Thank heaven you happened to be in the right place at the right time.'

'I'd come to fetch you any time if I thought you were in trouble.' He spoke softly, the words muffled against her cheek as he bent his head towards her. 'You know I would do anything for you, don't you? You only have to call and I'll be there.'

In her heart, she knew that was true. Why else was he here now? It made her feel warm all over to know that she could rely on him, and when he leaned towards her, as though he was about to kiss her, she wanted it more than anything.

His mouth brushed hers before settling gently on her lips, testing their softness, exploring the sweet fullness with tender, exhilarating thoroughness. Her lips parted, faintly trembling, clinging to his, wanting more.

'Mmm...sugar and spice and creamy coffee,' he murmured huskily. 'You taste delicious. You make me greedy for more...and more...and more.'

He deepened the kiss, drawing her into his arms so that her body meshed with his and she could feel the steady thud of his heartbeat against her own.

Kissing him was like drinking deeply of intoxicating wine. It went to her head and made her lose all sense of time and place, made her feel as though all that mattered was being here with him at this moment.

Then his hands moved over her, thrilling her with heated sensation, and all the while his fingers trailed and teased she was aware only of a fiery need to draw ever closer to him. Her breasts were softly crushed against his chest, her fingers tangled with the hair at the nape of his neck, and her lips were under siege, tingling with the sheer ecstasy of his passionate embrace.

She didn't know what it was that made her finally realise that reality was a lonely, dark road in the middle of the Scottish Highlands. Maybe it was the faint creak of leather upholstery, or the brush of the gear lever against her leg. Either way, she came back to the present with a sense of shock.

He must have latched on to similar thoughts, because he eased away from her a fraction and gazed around with a faintly bemused look in his eyes.

'Maybe we should start for home,' Izzy said, trying to gather her thoughts together. Now that her brain was starting to function again, she was beginning to wonder if she could blame her actions on the hot coffee. 'I don't know what I was thinking. It's almost as though the coffee was laced with alcohol. It went straight to my head.'

His brows shot up. 'Not guilty,' he said, and she realised that she must have actually spoken her thoughts aloud. 'I would never do anything like that. At least, I don't think I would. I suppose in the right circumstances I might resort to devious means.' He threw her a devilish smile.

'I'm sorry,' she said, her cheeks flushing with colour. 'I must have been talking to myself. It's just that everything that's happened this evening has been very unsettling. I can't think what came over me.'

'Put it down to a basic need for human companionship and comfort?' he suggested. 'We all suffer from that condition at some time or another.'

'Do we?' She studied him. 'You always seem so confident and in control. Nothing ever seems to faze you—even disputes with your father, or your brother, or the villagers. And now you're taking on the running of the estate, as well as holding down a job and looking after Alice's children.'

A momentary bleakness crossed his features. 'Eventually you learn to take most things in your stride. You deal with your problems and move on. It's the only way—as you've probably discovered.' He frowned. 'You didn't actually say how you came to be out here on this lonely road. Had you been out on a call?'

She nodded, a momentary recollection of her visit to the farmhouse filling her mind. 'Yes, to a farmhouse miles from anywhere.' Her gaze sparked with happiness. 'Oh, it was wonderful, Ross. One of the best things ever.'

A puzzled expression flitted across his face. 'Are you sure about that, given how it's turned out?' He laid a hand on her forehead, as though to check she was quite well, and then studied her curiously. 'Perhaps we ought to have you looked over at the hospital? You're obviously not thinking too clearly.'

'No, really—it's true.' She laughed. 'I delivered a baby—a little boy. He was absolutely gorgeous and it made me feel fantastic, on top of the world. I even got to wondering what it would be like to have a baby of my own to cuddle and love, just to share some of that heavenly feeling those new parents had when they were holding their baby in their arms.'

'Oh, I see.' He looked at her thoughtfully, taking in the blissful smile on her face, and then he said slowly, 'Well, we can do that. We can sort that out. Any time you like, I'm more than happy to oblige.' His arms closed around her, drawing her ever closer to him.

Her fingers tightened in her lap as his mischievous words washed over her, and her grey eyes shot flinty sparks in his direction. 'You are incredibly out of order, Ross Buchanan. Just because you've come out here to rescue me it doesn't mean you can start taking liberties that way. What happened just now was a mistake— because I was confused and needy. It won't happen again.'

'You don't really mean that, do you?' He gave her a look that was full of mock horror, a light dancing in his eyes that promised devilment and mayhem if ever he had the chance.

'Stop making fun of me. I'd appreciate it if you would drive me home, please.'

'Spoken like a truly well-mannered girl.' He was still laughing at her, but his hold on her relaxed. 'I will, of course—if you promise to come over to the castle after work tomorrow. The film crew are doing a run through of one of their main scenes in the Great Hall. They've agreed to let visitors view the proceedings. Lorna will be there, and one or two others. The GP, along with his wife and children, Mary from the shop, Maggie, of course, and the garage boss if he can get away. We're going to lay on some refreshments afterwards.'

The invitation brought her down to earth and gave her something to look forward to. Her eyes widened. 'How can I refuse? It sounds too good to miss. I've never seen a film in the making.'

'That's settled, then.' He made a crooked grin. 'Let's get this show on the road.' He snapped his seat belt into place and started up the car. 'You're welcome to ask your parents to come along, too, if you like. Your father might want to think of it as me extending an olive branch. I'd issue the invitation myself, but I can't be certain he would consider it.'

'Thanks,' she said, pleased that he had offered. 'That's a lovely gesture. I'll mention it, but I must say I really don't hold out too much hope. My father's a proud man, and it will take a lot for him to accept any invitation from you. You know he still hasn't been to see Alice in hospital? It's worrying me quite a bit.'

'I'm sorry about that.' He started to drive home. 'I was hoping that if Alice was released from hospital in time for Christmas he might consider inviting her to join your family for the celebrations. But that's probably not going to happen, is it?'

Izzy shook her head. 'My mother wants it, but he would never agree. She's tried coaxing him, but he just goes into stiff and starchy mode and won't even think about it.'

'It's depressing to think that he would hold a

grudge for such a long time.' He grimaced. 'But it doesn't matter. If she's well enough, I'll bring her to my place to recuperate. She'll be sad, though, because what she wants more than anything is to be accepted back into the fold.'

'I know.' It made Izzy unhappy to think of her cousin being ostracised this way. 'I've been racking my brain to see if I can find a way around it, but there doesn't seem to be a solution. The Buchanans are still his sworn enemy. What went on between him and your father, and his father before him, has had repercussions throughout the decades. Even thoughts of Alice's children won't melt his heart. He's only seen them briefly in passing since they've been here.'

He sent her a brief glance. 'I suppose it can't be helped. And Molly and Cameron don't seem to be too badly affected by any of this. I suppose it all tends to go over their heads. They haven't said anything about wanting to see him, although they *are* very fond of your mother. They call her Gran, and if your father happens to come into the conversation he's Grampops. I'm not quite sure how the name originated…whether it's a derivative of grandad, or poppa, or even grumpy gramps. I don't know, but it seems to have stuck.'

Izzy smiled at that. 'I know. I've heard them say it. I think it's meant to be a term of endearment. They don't know him, but they like him since he's associated with their gran.' She was thoughtful for a second or two. 'I'm sure he cares about them deep down…Alice, too. But he's been hurt by what he thinks of as her betrayal—of him and of the family name—and it's hard for him to reconcile that. I love my father, even though he can be difficult. He's a good man, but he can be immensely stubborn.'

'Perhaps he'll come round, given time.' Ross concentrated on the road ahead.

'I hope so.' She couldn't see it happening, though. It would probably take a miracle for her father to change his way of thinking. 'My mother told me that you've enrolled Molly and Cameron at the local school,' she said, changing the subject. 'How are they getting on?'

His mouth flattened. 'Not too well, by all

accounts. They've taken to the teachers, and they're quite happy with the work, but there's some friction with the other children. I suppose the animosity comes from their parents, who have a problem with me as the Laird. In turn the children take it with them to the playground. They get on well enough with Tom Slater's children, though, so I'm hoping things will settle down soon. Of course they'll be breaking up for the Christmas holidays very shortly.'

She looked at him, studying his face in the half-light. 'I think you've been great with the children. You've taken a lot on, taking care of them and Alice. I doubt other men would have been so keen to look after someone else's family.'

He turned the car onto the main road leading to the village. 'I think of them as *my* family... which they are through my brother. I feel responsible for them. It's no hardship to me to give them a home.'

Some time later he dropped her off at the cottage. He went straight home to relieve Maggie of the children, and Izzy went to soak for a while in a warm bath to ease her aching limbs. She'd taken quite a jolt when the car skidded, and she was already beginning to feel the after-effects.

'I heard about you being stranded,' Lorna said, when Izzy came down to the sitting room around an hour later, snug in a warm dressing gown and ready to sit in front of the cosy fire. 'I was going to come and find you myself, until the mechanic told me Ross had gone to help you out.' She picked up the remote control for the television. 'Did Ross tell you about the goings-on at the castle tomorrow?'

'He did. He said the producer has invited us along to watch the filming.'

Lorna nodded. 'Maggie told me that Ross asked specially if we could all come along. I think it's his way of trying to win the villagers over. It should be fun. I can't wait to see the actors doing their bit. You know one of them is Jason Trent, don't you? He was in that film about the Highland rebels last year. It broke box-office records. It makes me go hot all over, just thinking about him.'

Izzy was feeling a little feverish, too. But it wasn't Jason Trent who was stirring *her* blood. It was the memory of a close encounter in the front seat of a silver Range Rover that was causing her heart to race. Ross Buchanan had a lot to answer for, stirring her up body and soul, and what made it all worse was he was probably well aware of it.

He wasn't at the door to welcome them when she and Lorna arrived at the castle the next day. Instead Maggie, the housekeeper— middle-aged, friendly and straightforward in her manner—ushered them into the warm kitchen and offered them mulled wine and hors d'oeuvres.

'The place is bustling with activity,' she said. 'I've never known anything like it. So many folk under the roof at any one time. I think himself is taking on an awful lot—especially with the bairns running about the place.'

The children took over from Maggie as hosts as soon as they saw Izzy and Lorna.

'Come and see how they've set out the Great Hall,' Cameron said, racing ahead of them in his eagerness to be at the centre of things. 'They've put loads of food on the big table in there. It makes me hungry, looking at it, but the director says we have to wait a while—we can tuck in when the filming's finished, he says.'

'That's good, isn't it? None of that lovely food will go to waste.' Izzy smiled, glad to see the boy's excitement.

She was definitely impressed when she looked at the banqueting table. It had been laid with all manner of silverware, and with beautiful cande-labra and masses of food—turkey and hams, and great platters piled high with fruit.

'And all the actors and actresses are dressed up in old-fashioned clothes,' Molly put in. 'The ladies are wearing long skirts and blouses with lace at the cuffs, and some of them have shawls. They look really pretty.'

'I can't wait to see them,' Lorna said. 'Let's see if we can find a good place to view all the goings-on, shall we?'

'We can watch from up on the balcony,' Cameron told her. 'But we have to stay out of the way of the cameras and we have to be very quiet, or they'll have to do the film all over again. That's what the director said.'

They followed the children up the narrow staircase to the balcony overlooking the hall. 'Where's your uncle?' Lorna asked. 'Is he going to be joining us?'

'Yes,' Cameron answered briefly, 'in a few minutes.'

'He's showing Jason the broadsword from his collection,' Molly informed them importantly. 'He saw it hanging on the wall in the library and asked if he could look at it.'

'Men and their toys,' Lorna said, raising her eyes heavenward. 'I might have known.'

They joined the rest of the crowd who had come to view the filming, chatting amicably among themselves until the director called for quiet and the actors began to take their places.

The setting was a banquet, where people were gathered around the table eating, drinking, and generally merrymaking. Lorna's heartthrob took up position at the foot of the staircase, where he was talking to the lady of the house, and all was pleasant, homely interchange. Soon, though, he swivelled around to face a Highland clansman who had erupted into the hall from a door at the far side of the room. The lady moved hurriedly out of range, alarmed by the intruder.

'You'll pay for the deed you've done this day,' the Highlander said, advancing menacingly towards Jason. 'I'm here to avenge my kinsman.'

From then on it was truly as though they were witnessing a fiery feud. It was so realistic that at one point Molly hid behind Izzy, only risking a peek at the scene through one eye. Cameron's expression was awestruck, but he, too, sidled closer to Izzy.

The intruder, whose dark hair flowed with every flourish, was dressed in full Scottish regalia: kilt, loose linen shirt and waistcoat, and an impressive woollen cloak that swung importantly with every movement. Now he rushed towards the stairs with such realistic energy that the gathered crowd instinctively moved back. They could not be seen, of course, by the camera lens, since they were way above the line of view.

As the action progressed the two actors engaged in a magnificent tussle which took them halfway up the staircase. The intruder was thrown against the balustrade, and seemed to be almost done for, but then he came back at his opponent, brandishing his sword.

'Cut!' the director called, and all action ceased. 'That was great,' he said. 'Take a break, everyone. We'll do the scene outside the walls in half an hour.'

Ross appeared from a side door and waved up at Izzy and Lorna, beckoning them to come down. 'I'll introduce you to Jason and Murray,' he said.

Izzy checked that the children were all right, and not too shaken up by their experience.

'Wow!' Cameron said, brandishing an imaginary sword. 'I can do that.' He brandished his invisible weapon and chased his sister along the balcony.

Izzy went to rescue her. 'What did you think

of the acting?' she asked. 'Do you think it was a bit scary?'

Molly thought about it. 'A bit.' She gave a wide smile. 'It looked ever so real.'

'I wonder if we can go and eat some of the food now?' Cameron wanted to know.

They trooped downstairs. Jason and Lorna hit it off right away, and after a few minutes moved off together in the direction of an ante-room. Izzy glanced at Lorna, lifting a brow, and Lorna made a 'go away and don't disturb me now' gesture with her hand, making Izzy chuckle.

She turned her attention back to Ross and Murray, the actor who played the part of the intruder, and Murray explained the storyline behind the action they had just witnessed.

'I think it's going to be a great film,' Izzy told him. 'It was so powerful—and colourful, too. Of course the setting's just right.'

'Can we eat now?' Cameron said in a plaintive tone. 'I can't just keep looking at all that food. Besides, everyone else is helping themselves, and Maggie is handing out drinks.'

'You're so greedy,' Molly remonstrated with him. 'Anybody would think you haven't had anything to eat today.'

Cameron pondered that. 'That was an hour ago,' he said. 'It wasn't pastry and it doesn't count.'

Molly shook her head like a wise little old lady. 'Boys,' she said.

Ross chuckled. 'Go and have something to eat,' he said. He looked back at Murray. 'What about you? Shall we go and help ourselves?'

Murray hesitated. 'Perhaps in a while,' he murmured. 'You go ahead. I'll just stay here for a minute and think about my next scene.'

Izzy looked at him closely. 'Are you all right?' she asked. 'Only I've noticed you seem to be moving a bit stiffly since filming finished. Were you hurt during the fight scene?'

'It's just a bruise, I imagine,' he said. 'One of the hazards of the job. The action gets a bit fierce sometimes.'

'Like when you were thrown onto the balustrade?' Ross suggested. 'I thought you landed heavily. It looked too realistic to have been manufactured.'

Murray grinned crookedly. 'You're right about that.' He caught his breath. 'I think I'll just go and get some air,' he said.

He started to move away, and Izzy glanced at Ross. 'Do you think we should follow him?' she asked. 'He looks a bit winded to me. I'm not sure he's as okay as he says he is.'

Ross nodded. 'I'll suggest that we go into the library. Maybe he'll let me take a look at him there. I keep my medical bag in there, so it'll be handy if we need it.'

He went and spoke quietly to Maggie, letting her know what they were doing.

'That's all right. I'll watch the children for you,' she said. There was a faint affectionate smile in her eyes as she spoke, and Izzy could see that Maggie was warming to Ross. He was making conquests all round, it seemed. It was just a pity that her father wasn't to be counted among them.

Murray agreed to go with Izzy and Ross to the library. Izzy guessed that he wanted to be able to sit somewhere for a while, away from prying eyes. He appeared to be uncomfortable and increasingly breathless.

'Sit yourself down,' Ross said, indicating a comfortable leather-backed chair. 'How are you feeling?'

'Not so good,' Murray said. He began to cough, and clutched at his side.

'I'm wondering if you might have damaged something when you fell against the balustrade,' Ross murmured. 'Would you let me have a look at you? Izzy's a doctor, too, so maybe she could offer a second opinion if we need one?'

Murray nodded, sitting down. 'It's a sharp pain,' he said. 'I'm thinking I might have broken a rib or two.'

'I'll get my medical bag,' Ross said.

Izzy went to stand beside Murray and took his pulse. He was looking increasingly ill as the minutes went by, and his breathing was becoming rapid.

'His pulse is rapid, but weak,' she told Ross when he came back with his medical bag. 'And the veins in his neck are beginning to swell.' That wasn't a good sign. It meant that pressure was building up inside the chest cavity.

By now Murray was showing signs of anxiety and distress, and she set about soothing him while Ross took a blood pressure reading.

'Blood pressure's falling,' Ross said, 'and there are decreased breath sounds in the lung.' He started to remove equipment from his medical case while Izzy explained to Murray what was happening.

'It looks as though you're right about the broken ribs,' she told him. 'Normally you would just be given painkilling medication to help you through that, but because of your other symptoms it seems that one of the ribs has punctured the lung. That means that air has gone into your chest cavity and can't escape, so it's pressing on the lung, causing it to collapse and making you breathless.'

This was a medical emergency. Murray looked near to collapse, and if they didn't remove the trapped air and restore function to his lung he could soon start to suffer heart failure and go into cardiac arrest.

'I'm going to put a tube into your chest to remove

the trapped air,' Ross said. 'As soon as that's done you should start to feel more comfortable.'

'Do you want me to anaesthetise the area while you prepare?' Izzy asked.

Ross nodded. 'Thanks. I'll set up a bottle with fluid to act as a valve to prevent the air returning.' He glanced at Murray. 'We'll put one end of the tube in your chest, and the other end in the fluid in the bottle.'

Izzy carefully infiltrated a local anaesthetic into the area, checking all the time that Murray was coping with the procedure.

'I'm doing okay,' he managed.

'Good,' Izzy said, giving him a reassuring smile.

Ross made an incision in Murray's chest and carefully inserted the tube. There was a satisfying hiss of escaping air, and he sealed the end of the tube in the bottle valve. Murray's breathing began to improve almost immediately, and Izzy gave a soft sigh of relief.

'You're out of the woods,' she said, laying a hand lightly on his shoulder.

Murray's tense expression slowly evaporated as

he became more comfortable. 'That feels so much better,' he said. 'Thanks, Ross—and you, too, Izzy.' He looked into her eyes. 'You have the hands of an angel and a beautiful soothing voice. You can come and take care of me any time you like.'

Ross gave him a mock-stern look. 'Don't you be getting any ideas on that score,' he said, feigning antagonism. 'You actors have something of a reputation where women are concerned, don't you? But I'm telling you, Izzy's out of bounds.'

Murray sent him a rueful smile. 'Possessive, are you? Staking a claim? Now, there's a thing. Seems to me she's a woman worth fighting for. I'm inclined not to give up so easily—warning or no.'

'You can both stop dreaming right now and come back down to earth,' Izzy said in a blunt tone. 'This is no time to be fooling around. We have to get you to hospital, Murray, to be X-rayed and monitored. And on another point, for your information, *neither* of you is on my list of eligible bachelors.'

And it was just as well to remind herself of

that. Because she was getting way too fond of Ross—and it wouldn't do, would it, given all the upheaval it would cause in her family?

CHAPTER EIGHT

'I WOULDN'T be at all surprised if we had more snowfall some time today. The wind's getting up, too.' Lorna was frowning as she looked out of the window of the cottage. 'It doesn't make for a promising outlook for your journey to Inverness, does it?'

'I suppose not. But Alice is so thrilled at the prospect of coming home at last. I wouldn't dream of disappointing her—or the children.' Izzy drew out a batch of mince pies from the oven and a satisfying aroma of spices filled the kitchen. 'Ross said we would go over to the hospital and fetch her this morning, and with any luck we'll be back before things get too bad. I just hope everyone who has to travel home for Christmas gets there safely. This is not a good time of year for things to go wrong, is it?'

'No, it isn't.' Lorna turned away from the window. 'I was planning on going over to my parents' house to spend Christmas Day with them. It would be an awful blow if we were to be snowed in and I couldn't get there, wouldn't it? I thought I might take the train, actually. It might be simpler. My mother does us proud every year…there's so much lovely food that we're stuffed for the rest of the day.' Lorna frowned. 'I don't think I could contemplate not getting there.'

'Too true. I suppose if that did happen, though, you could always come over and spend the day with my family.' Izzy laid out the pies to cool on a rack. 'Unless, of course, you get an invitation to share Christmas with Jason Trent,' she added. 'I heard you and he were planning on having a meal together at a posh restaurant this weekend. It sounds as though things are heating up for you two.'

Lorna's eyes widened. 'Word soon gets

around, doesn't it? I thought we'd kept that pretty much to ourselves. We didn't want the whole neighbourhood talking about it. Next thing the press will be hanging around, taking photos.'

Izzy studied her briefly. 'Then he shouldn't have told Murray about it. A nurse overheard them chatting, and now it's the talk of the hospital.' She laughed. 'Maybe you'll have to change the venue.'

'Too right.' Lorna smiled ruefully. 'I should have known.' She took a bite out of a mince pie. 'Mmm…these are delicious—hot, though.' She grinned, savouring the pastry. 'Murray's doing all right after his nasty accident, isn't he? He said they've filmed all his major scenes, and he'll be able to get by with the ones that are left because there's nothing too strenuous involved—only some dialogue and a bit of canoodling with one of the leading ladies. Greg said he had the luck of the devil, and your Alice laughed and said she hadn't realised Greg was the jealous type. She's been teasing him ever since, apparently.'

Izzy smiled, shaking icing sugar on to the golden crust of the pies. 'It sounds as though she's pretty much back on form, doesn't it? She's still unsteady on her feet, but I'm sure that will remedy itself given time.'

'She's lucky to have done as well as she has, by all accounts.' Lorna was looking at the mince pies, debating whether to have another one. 'The crash left her with head injuries and spinal contusions, didn't it? As well as a host of other things? She's a miracle of modern medical science.' She reached for another temptingly aromatic pie.

'You're right. I can't wait to see her properly up and about again.'

The doorbell rang, and Izzy went to answer it, expecting Ross. Instead she found her parents waiting there. She hugged each of them in turn and invited them into the house.

'We came to bring Christmas presents for Lorna to take home with her, and I wanted to make sure you knew what our arrangements were,' her mother said. 'You *are* going to come to us for Christmas dinner, aren't you? Your grandparents will be there, along with your aunt and uncle.'

'Of course,' Izzy said, showing them into the kitchen. 'I've just baked a batch of pies to bring over to you. That's if there are any left after Lorna has finished dipping into them.' She grinned, and Lorna put a hand to her mouth as though to hide her guilt.

'Oops,' she said. 'Mind you, Izzy did make quite a lot. She said she was going to take a few over to Alice.'

'I thought she might appreciate a few home comforts,' Izzy said. 'Just to get her in the mood for Christmas.'

'Of course—you're bringing her home today, aren't you?' her mother said.

Izzy nodded. 'Ross is coming to pick me up in a while.' Out of the corner of her eye she was aware of her father stiffening, and her spirits sank.

'I expect the children must be over the moon.' Her mother took no notice of her husband's attitude but smiled, clearly thinking about the reunion.

'They are,' Izzy murmured. 'But I'm not so sure that they're going to be too keen on the journey there and back to fetch her. You know how it is with youngsters being cooped up in a car. They've made the drive several times, and they get very restless. Maggie was going to look after them, but she has to see to her own family and do some last-minute Christmas shopping, with the great day being just a short time away.'

'I would have kept them here with me,' Lorna said, 'but I have to go to work this afternoon. I think Ross was hoping that he might find a baby-sitter. Last I heard, he hadn't told the children that today's the day.'

Izzy's mother glanced towards her husband. 'I wouldn't mind looking after them.'

'We can't do that,' he said. 'You know we're going to visit your father. He's not been well.'

'It's only a cold, Stuart,' her mother retorted. 'You're just making excuses.'

'I don't need to make excuses,' he answered. 'You know how I feel about the situation. Every day Buchanan does something to remind me of what's gone on in the past. He's even brought more earth-moving equipment onto his land in the last few days. It was holding up the traffic again a couple of days ago. What's he planning on doing with it, do you think? He's having more foundations dug out, I'll be bound. He'll have a fight on his hands if I find he's gone against the planning regulations. Is he *determined* to take away my business?'

Izzy frowned. 'I thought the building work was pretty much finished,' she said. 'Maybe he's brought the equipment in to help with the tree-planting? I know he wanted to put in some mature trees on one part of the estate to provide a barrier against the wind. They can be pretty hefty, from what I've heard, and need large cavities for the roots. And he also mentioned shoring up the land in some parts to act as a flood barrier on one area of the estate.'

'Hmmph. There's not much likelihood of that happening on *my* part of the river, is there? I'm sure he's damming it upstream.'

She could see her father wasn't convinced by

any alternative explanation she tried to give. The doorbell rang again, and Izzy contemplated how she was going to manage the situation with her father and Ross in the same room. It was difficult, being plunged into the role of peacemaker, and it was something she would much rather do without.

Molly and Cameron were full of news about their plans for the day. 'We're going to the doctor's house,' they told her. 'Mrs Slater says she'll take us shopping. She says she has to buy some food for Christmas, so we're going to help her choose it, and we can pick out some goodies for *our* celebrations.'

Izzy glanced at Ross. 'So you found a solution, then?'

He nodded. 'That's right… And I managed to find a wheelchair for Alice, too.' He glanced briefly at the children. 'Luckily I hadn't mentioned any other happenings, so there are no problems there.'

'That's good.' Their comments appeared to have gone over the top of the children's heads, but now she signalled with her eyes towards the kitchen. 'My parents are here.' It was the least she could do to warn him.

Izzy led the way into the kitchen. 'Ross has managed to find a wheelchair for Alice, for when she comes home,' she told her parents.

'I'm glad you thought of that,' her mother said, smiling at Ross. 'I was a little worried about how she was going to manage.' She studied him thoughtfully. 'You've been very kind to her, bringing her to the hospital in Inverness and making sure that she's all right.'

Izzy's father made an exasperated sound. 'Does it not occur to you that his conscience is driving him? How is it that Alice came to be in the hospital in the first place?'

'My mummy had an accident in the car,' Molly piped up in all innocence, as though she was explaining to someone who knew nothing of what had gone on. 'Uncle Ross looked after her and he called the ambulance.'

Stuart McKinnon looked uncomfortable, a frown etching itself on his brow and his mouth turning down a fraction at the corners. He probably hadn't expected a small child to take any note of what he was saying.

'Would you children like to come and see the decorations we've put up in the living room?' Lorna suggested hurriedly, obviously sensing trouble brewing. 'We've decorated the tree with gold and silver baubles. I think it looks lovely.'

The children followed her, happily unaware of any tension in the atmosphere and eager to inspect the Christmas trimmings. As soon as they had gone, Morag McKinnon turned on her husband. 'How could you say such a thing—and in front of the bairns, too?'

His shoulders moved in an awkward gesture. 'I speak as I find. Would you have me do otherwise?' He looked directly at Ross. 'It has to be guilt that's driving you. You were there when the accident happened. It was probably you that caused it, with your constant arguments with your brother. The fact that he ran off with your girlfriend must have stuck in your craw. Perhaps that's why you were following them. Everyone knows that you were driving behind them on the day of the accident. Maybe they were trying to get away from you. You're most likely the reason that Alice is in hospital.'

Ross studied him for a long moment. 'From the way you're talking, anyone would imagine that you are concerned about what happened to Alice,' he said. 'If that's the case, why haven't you been to visit her? Why haven't you tried to reconcile your differences with her? You looked after Alice as though she was your own daughter for years, and yet the instant she went against you you abandoned her—you cast her off as though she meant nothing to you.'

He frowned. 'Since she's been injured, you haven't made any attempt to visit her, or to make arrangements for where she's to stay on her release from hospital. I don't see any vestige of love in that kind of response. So why should you care either way about my involvement with her?'

'I don't.' Izzy's father started to walk towards the door, his expression dark as a thundercloud.

Izzy felt a pang of anguish as he threw a backward glance towards her mother. Would this feud never end? Could these two men never be in the same room together without arguing?

'We should go, Morag,' he said abruptly. 'Your father will be expecting us.' He went out into the hall and out of the front door.

Izzy's mother watched him leave, and hesitated before sending Ross an apologetic look. 'I know this isn't your fault, Ross, and I hope you will try to understand—he has great difficulty coming to terms with what happened. Alice left without a word, without giving us any indication of where she was going, and she didn't get in touch afterwards for a long, long time. We had to rely on other people to tell us what was going on. She knew how we felt about her being with your brother, and I think it really hurt Izzy's father that she didn't try to talk to him about it.'

She pulled in a deep breath. 'I know why she did what she did, of course. He can be brusque and inflexible and very hard to approach. But underneath it all he cares very deeply. I know he's torn. On the one hand he blames her for leaving with the son of his lifelong enemy, and on the other he feels that she was like a daughter to him and she let him down. I don't know how to break down that barrier. I wish I could. I hate to see him hurting, and it grieves me to see Alice suffer, too.'

'I understand, Morag.' Ross gave a brief nod of acknowledgement, his mouth making a faint downturn. 'But he has to find a way to get over his antagonism before it destroys him. It's gone on for too long through the generations, and it's even affecting Alice's children at school—with youngsters pointing the finger at them. They don't deserve any of this. I'm not going to stand by and see them vilified for what went on in the past.'

Molly and Cameron came into the room. 'There's a beautiful star at the top of the tree,' Molly told Izzy's mother. 'It sparkles, and you can see lots of different coloured lights in it.'

'I like the lanterns,' Cameron said. 'They're all shiny and bright, and they kind of float in the air. Lorna says when you open the door they start to twirl.'

'I've seen them,' Morag said. 'They're very

pretty.' She gave each of the children a quick cuddle, and then said, 'I must go. We're off to see Izzy's grandad. He's been poorly.'

'I want to give Grampops our card,' Molly said. 'We made it for him for Christmas.'

'We made one for you, as well,' Cameron said, handing a homemade card to Izzy's mother. 'Maggie helped us to make them. I stuck the sparkly baubles on the tree—see? They're a bit crooked, but they look pretty, don't they?'

'I think it's a beautiful card,' Morag said, deeply touched. 'Thank you very much, both of you. I shall put it on my mantelpiece where everyone can see it.'

The children beamed happily and followed her to the door. Izzy's father stood outside, a solitary figure waiting by a tree.

Molly went over to him, looking up at him in a puzzled fashion. 'Are you cross?' she asked. 'You look cross.'

'No, Molly,' he said looking down at her. 'I'm not cross with you.'

'Good.' She gave him a wide smile. 'Sometimes you look as though you're a bit sad,' she said, 'so I've made you a card. Well, me and Cameron made it together. It's Santa Claus. He's got a big smile on his face and he makes everyone happy.' She thrust the card into his hands. 'Happy Christmas, Grampops.'

He took the card she offered, holding it in his hands as he looked down at the brightly coloured Santa, with a cotton wool beard and cherry-red cheeks. He swallowed hard, and for a moment Izzy thought his eyes misted over. He blinked, though, and straightened up, saying huskily, 'Thank you for that, both of you. That was very thoughtful of you. Thank you very much.'

He patted Cameron awkwardly on his shoulder, and would have done the same to Molly—except that she reached up and hugged him as tightly as she could, and he wavered for a moment before folding his arms around her briefly.

When she let go and stood back he gave the children an uneasy wave of his hand and went over to his car. He didn't say anything more, and it occurred to Izzy that he was overcome by the simple, generous affection of a small child who knew nothing of the troubles of the adult world.

After they had gone, Izzy turned to walk back into the house and was startled to see Ross standing at the door. He didn't say anything, but laid an arm around each of the children and led them slowly back to the kitchen.

'You should say goodbye to Lorna,' he said to them eventually. 'It's time we were setting off for the doctor's house. He'll be waiting for you.'

He looked at Izzy, his expression thoughtful, his manner somehow subdued. 'Lorna's put a few of those mince pies in a box for you to take to Alice,' he said. 'If we leave now, we might just miss the storm. They say there'll likely be a blizzard towards evening, and I want to have Alice back home safely before then.'

Izzy nodded and went to get her coat. A short time later they dropped off the children at the doctor's house and set off on their journey to Inverness.

The roads were fairly clear, although there was still snow lying around on the grass verges and over the fields, and the traffic moved at a fairly rapid pace. Izzy was glad of that, because it meant they would reach Alice all the sooner. Even so, she was a little worried about the weather conditions. The roads were slippery, and though it didn't matter, since they were driving in Ross's roadworthy vehicle, she was wary of how the conditions might affect other drivers.

Ross didn't take any chances, though. He drove steadily and carefully, and after a while she began to relax. 'I'm sorry for what my father said,' she told him. 'I know my mother has tried to reason with him over the years, but it has been difficult for her—for all of us. I suppose he remembers how his great-aunt died in childbirth, and how the family grieved and mourned her loss for so many years. They blamed the Buchanan who abandoned her as soon as he found she was pregnant, and things have gone from bad to worse ever since then.'

'I realise that we're all tarred with the same brush,' Ross said. 'I have the same problem justifying my position with the villagers.

There's always a wealth gap, and resentment that my family own the land that they're living on. I'm doing what I can to run the estate in a way that will eventually be beneficial for the whole community, but I doubt anyone will appreciate that.'

'I'm sure Alice appreciates what you've done for her. She told me she's so happy to be coming home, and even happier to know that you've provided a place for her and her children.'

He sent her an oblique glance. 'I know that's what Robert would have wanted,' he said. 'He was planning on coming back here at some point to show his children where he was born. I don't think he wanted to live at the castle, but he thought the lodge might provide decent living accommodation when it was finally finished. That's why I've been trying to push on with the work—to make sure that it's ready for Alice and the children. I think for a while, though, she'll want to stay with me and Maggie, so that we can look after her until she's properly back on her feet.'

Izzy smiled at him, thankful for the way he

cared, but her lips stiffened and her smile froze as they rounded a bend in the road. Ahead of them a car had spun around in a wide arc that even now was etched out on the sleet-covered road. Another car had run into it. It looked as though the first car had swerved to avoid another, after taking the bend too wide.

Someone was desperately trying to direct traffic away from the crashed vehicles, and at least the accident had happened far enough away from the bend for oncoming traffic to avoid more tragedy. Other people were trying to push the vehicles onto the verge, out of harm's way.

'We should stop and see if anyone is hurt,' Izzy said, but Ross was already slowing down and steering his vehicle onto the verge some distance beyond the crashed cars.

'I'll get my medical bag,' he said.

Izzy climbed out of the car and went over to the side of the road to see if she could help in any way.

'We've called the police and the ambulance,' a man told her. 'There are a couple of people who are badly injured—a man and a woman. Both of them are still in the car. I think it's bad. The two people from the other car managed to get out. I've made them sit back out of the way until help comes. I don't know what to do for the others.'

'My friend and I are both doctors,' Izzy said. 'We'll take a look at them and see what we can do before the ambulance gets here.'

She quickly discovered that the man still in the car was the one who needed immediate attention. 'I think he has an abdominal injury,' she told Ross, meeting up with him. 'The other injured person is a woman, Carol, with a broken leg and possible spinal injuries.'

Ross didn't speak, and she glanced at him to see if he had heard what she'd said. He was white-faced, his expression shocked, and he walked stiffly towards the vehicle were the people were trapped, almost as though it was taking everything in him to do what he had to do.

Izzy spoke to the injured man, trying to see if he was able to describe any specific damage, but he was fading in and out of consciousness the whole time. It was clear that the steering column had twisted on impact and caused at least one of his injuries.

She checked his vital signs and said quietly, 'His blood pressure is low and his heart-rate is way too high. We need to get him on oxygen and put in an intravenous line so that we can give him painkillers and fluids. I can do that while you splint Carol's leg.'

Ross didn't answer, and she glanced at him once more. There was a faint sheen of perspiration on his forehead and he looked as though he was going to be sick at any minute.

'Are you all right?' she asked. 'I can do this if you need to go and take a few minutes.'

He looked around at the wreckage, and the incline of the road where it skirted the hillside. Then he pulled in a deep breath and nodded. 'I'm fine,' he said. 'I'll put in the IV line while you start the oxygen. Then one of us should go and get some splints from my car.'

She guessed that he was suffering from a feeling of *déjà vu*. Was this how it had been when his brother and Alice had suffered their dreadful injuries?

'You'll need to put a pressure pad on the woman's leg to control the bleeding,' he said after a while. 'Do you want to check in my bag? There should be everything we need in there.'

'I'll see to it.' She glanced at him once again. He seemed to be coping, doing what was necessary to stabilise the injured man, and she concentrated her attention on the woman.

'I'm going to put a supportive collar around your neck,' she told her. 'We won't know what damage has been done until we can get you to the hospital for X-rays and scans.'

'What about John?' the woman asked, her voice shaky. 'He's not speaking. How is he doing?'

'He's breathing, and we've given him pain medication so he won't be too uncomfortable,' Izzy said. 'It's possible that he has some internal injuries, so we need to get him to hospital as soon as possible. We'll put both of you on spinal boards, to make sure that there's no chance of further injury while we take you there.'

Ambulance sirens sounded in the distance, and Izzy left the patients with Ross while she went to confer with the paramedics. Just a minute later a fire engine arrived, and the crew started to assess how best they could remove the patients from the mangled vehicle.

By now they had done all that they could for the man and woman inside the car. The two injured people who were sitting on the verge appeared to have escaped with minor injuries, but Ross still knelt down beside them and checked them out.

'You'll be given a more thorough examination in the Accident and Emergency department at the hospital,' he told them. 'For the moment it seems as though you have some bruising and pulled ligaments. We can make you more comfortable with support bandages.' He turned to the young man, who was nursing a sore shoulder. 'It looks as though you might have broken your collarbone. I'll put a sling around your arm and that should ease things for you.'

Izzy worked with him to put dressings on cuts

and apply bandages to sprains. It wasn't too long before the fire crew indicated that it was safe to remove the man and woman from their car, and both Izzy and Ross went to supervise their transfer to spinal boards and then to the first ambulance.

A few minutes later the ambulance was on its way, siren blaring, heading for Accident and Emergency. Izzy went to help the walking injured into the second vehicle, while Ross spoke with the police officer who had come to investigate.

It was some time before Izzy and Ross went back to Ross's car. Ross sat in the driving seat, his whole body stiff and very still. He didn't speak but simply stared ahead.

'Would you like me to drive?' Izzy asked. 'You don't seem to be yourself. Ever since we came upon this accident it's as though you've been knocked for six.' She was concerned about him. He had hardly spoken the whole time they were with the accident victims, except to reassure them and ask relevant questions. He was still pale, and now he was gripping the steering wheel, his fingers wrapped tightly around it so that his knuckles were white. 'Is this something to do with what happened to Robert and Alice?'

He nodded. 'Everything is so similar,' he said. 'Almost as though it might have been this same stretch of road. Of course it wasn't. But the hillside, the blind curve, and then that straight road ahead…it's exactly as it was.'

He paused, shuddering a little, and Izzy said, 'I guessed that might be the case. You've never really spoken about it. What happened? Do you want to tell me?'

He was silent for a moment or two, and then he said quietly, 'I was on my way to work, and I was following them as they were heading towards Alice's sister's house. They were going to fetch the children, and they were looking forward to telling them about their plans for the future. Summer was just beginning, and Robert was thinking of coming back home. Alice was hoping that she might persuade your father to accept her back into the family.'

He pressed his lips together in a grim line. 'And then a car came out of nowhere, trying to overtake. It smashed into them, and all their dreams dissolved in an instant.'

'You saw it all? I know you must have. You were injured, too, weren't you?' Izzy frowned, wanting to comfort him yet at the same time knowing he needed to say this in his own way, to bring it all out into the open.

'I was afraid I was going to hit them. I slammed on my brakes, and tried to swerve out of the way. It all happened so fast. I remember a jolt, and I hit a tree so hard that the side of my car crumpled and I broke some ribs. I couldn't think of anything except that I needed to get to Robert and Alice, that I had to check on the others. There were two other cars involved, and people were injured in all of them. I did what I could, but it wasn't enough to save Robert. He took the worst of the impact.'

A muscle in his jaw tightened, and she could see that he was trying to bring himself under control. She laid a hand on his arm, stroking gently, wanting desperately to take him into her arms and hold him.

He drew in a ragged breath. 'All Robert could think about was Alice. He begged me to take care of her, to make sure that she came out of it safe and sound. I told him that I would take care of her, and he said, "The children, too. They should see their heritage."'

He looked at her. 'I told him that he needn't worry about any of it, that all he had to do was stay with us, and he said, 'I'm sorry. I know they'll be in good hands.'

Izzy reached for him, her arms going around him, and he leaned towards her, sliding his arms around her waist, resting his head against her breast. 'You kept your promise to your brother,' she whispered. 'No one could have asked you to do more.'

He gave a ragged sigh, and she stroked his thick, springy hair, offering what comfort she could. Was this the first time he had played it all out in his mind? Probably not, but today's accident must have brought it back to him with shocking clarity.

'Perhaps now you can begin to come to terms

with everything that happened?' she murmured. 'You have to look to the future and make sure that the Buchanan name rings with pride. Surely the best thing you can do to preserve Robert's memory is to bring the estate to its full potential and make it an emblem of all that is good for the community.'

She hesitated. 'I'm sure Alice and the children will thank you for that, and you've already made a start with your plans for the winery. That will provide work for the villagers, and maybe it will stop some of the younger ones leaving for the towns.'

'You could be right.' His breath shuddered in his throat, his shoulders moving as he tightened his hold on her, pressing her to him. 'We have to move on and put the past behind us.'

They stayed like that, wrapped in each other's arms, for a long time, both of them quiet, thinking about what had gone before.

Then Ross straightened, drawing back from her. 'We should go and fetch Alice,' he said. 'It's time to bring her home.'

He started up the engine, setting the car in motion once more.

Izzy sank back against the upholstery of her seat and tried to let the image of that terrible accident fade from her mind. It was no easy thing to do, and for Ross, who had witnessed it and been part of it, the torment must have returned in full force.

He had borne all that had happened with a stoicism that would put others to shame. He was a good man, a strong man with deep-seated principles and a streak of pride that ran through every pore. Beneath that tough, devil-may-care exterior he cared intensely for his family, and he would never let them down.

She knew it with certainty—just as she realised with a sense of shock and wonder that he was the one man, the only man, she could ever love.

Somewhere along the way he had stolen her heart.

CHAPTER NINE

'IT'S so wonderful to be going home,' Alice said, sitting in a chair at the side of her bed and looking around the ward for the last time.

Izzy gathered up the last of her belongings, putting them all together by the wheelchair Ross had brought with them. She glanced at Alice. Her tawny hair was the same shade as Molly's, with wispy curls framing her face, and her green eyes were shining with relief at the thought of leaving the hospital. It was good to see her looking so happy.

'I'll come and see you just as soon as you're settled at Ross's place,' Greg said, coming to take Alice's hand in his. 'I'd have taken you home with me, except that I'm working the late shift today. I just had to come and see you off, though.'

'I'm glad you came,' Alice told him. 'It's been great to have a friend working here all the time I've been confined to this place. Thanks so much for all you've done.'

'You're very welcome,' Greg murmured, helping her into the wheelchair. 'Make sure you take it easy once you get home. You've still some recuperating to do, so no burning the midnight oil or trying to dance the Highland Reel.'

'Oh, I'm bound to do that, aren't I?' Alice chuckled. 'The most I can manage at the moment is a bit of a totter—though maybe after I've sampled some of Ross's fruit wines, anything might be possible.'

'I can see Izzy's been telling you tales,' Ross said, smiling. 'Don't believe a word of it. The wines are mildly intoxicating. You might find walking in a straight line a bit difficult afterwards, that's all.'

'Or, then again, *reel* might be a more appropriate word,' Izzy put in. 'I believe Greg had it right the first time.'

'You're quite mad, all of you,' Alice said,

laughing. 'I'm really looking forward to seeing Molly and Cameron at home, away from these antiseptic conditions, and the thought of looking out over the beautiful mountains and lochs is enough to keep me going for a long time.'

'That's good. Let's get on our way, then, shall we?' Ross took hold of the wheelchair and started to guide it out of the side ward.

Alice waved goodbye to Greg, and Izzy stayed behind to speak to him for a moment, saying, 'I'll catch you both up in a minute or two.'

'You're worried about the people who came in by ambulance, aren't you?' Greg said. 'I didn't mention anything to Alice about them. I thought it might be a bit too traumatic.'

Izzy nodded. 'I know they came to you in A&E. How are they doing? Have you managed to assess them completely, yet?'

'We have. As you expected, the woman has a broken femur, which we've put right under anaesthetic. She'll be wearing a plaster cast for some time, so Christmas is going to be a little awkward for her. As to John, he's not so lucky.

There was damage to his spleen and liver, so he's undergoing surgery at the moment. It looks as though he'll be staying in hospital for a week or two—at least until the New Year.'

'That doesn't seem so far away now, does it? One and a half weeks? I still have shopping to do and preparations to make.'

'I thought you were going to your parents' house for Christmas?' He raised a questioning brow.

'I am, but there's a lot for my mother to cope with, so I thought I'd help out by making a few things... A quiche and some sausage rolls, maybe some hors d'oeuvres.'

'Alice would love it...all that home cooking. I don't suppose there's any chance your father will see sense and invite her along, is there?'

Izzy shook her head. 'I don't think so. To be honest, I half wish I could get away and join her at Ross's place, but I don't want to upset my mother...or my father, come to that. And I think Maggie will make sure there's a feast on hand—and Ross will do everything he can to make her happy.'

'She'll be thankful to be with Molly and Cameron, anyway. I might suggest to Ross that I go round and pay a visit in the afternoon on Christmas Day. I come from a large family and they won't miss me too much by teatime. Do you think Ross would mind?'

'I shouldn't think so. Best thing would be to ask him and judge by his reaction.'

She took her leave of Greg and hurried to catch up with Ross and Alice. Would Ross want to keep Alice all to himself? It was hard for her to say. How much did Ross still care for her cousin? And how much of his thoughtfulness could be put down to his sense of responsibility towards her or to the honouring of a promise made to his brother?

Was there any chance that Ross might have some deeper feeling for her, Izzy? He had hinted as much, but she could never be sure that he wasn't teasing her or playing her along. The trouble was, she wanted him to care deeply. Suddenly it was the most important thing in the world to her.

They arrived back at the castle by late afternoon. Izzy stayed with Alice and helped her to settle in, while Ross went to fetch Molly and Cameron from the doctor's house.

There was huge excitement when they ran indoors and found their mother waiting for them.

'We didn't know you were coming home,' Cameron said, his eyes wide. 'No one told us.'

'We thought it would be a great surprise for you,' Ross said. 'But we have to take good care of your mother now that she's home. So you won't be able to rush around near her because if she's not sitting in the wheelchair she'll need to be very careful how she gets about. She still has to learn how to walk properly.'

'We'll be good as good,' Molly exclaimed. She went over to her mother and gave her an enormous hug. 'I'm so glad that you're home,' she said.

Izzy left shortly after that. 'It looks as though the wind is getting up now,' she told Ross, 'and I want to be home before it sets in.'

'I'll drive you,' Ross offered, but she shook her head.

'You stay with Alice. I'll walk. It will help to

clear my head. Somehow today has been a lot more intense than I expected. It must be the excitement of bringing Alice home.'

He went with her to the door, and as she would have left to go on her way he wrapped his arms around her and held her close. 'I'm glad that you were with me today,' he murmured. 'There was a point where I thought I couldn't go on, and you brought me back to face up to everything that was real and important. Thank you for that. I haven't been able to talk to anybody properly about what happened, and it was good that you were there, that you listened.'

He lowered his head and kissed her tenderly on the lips. It was a beautiful, sweet sensation, being folded in his arms that way, having him kiss her as though he really cared about her. She wanted it to go on and on for ever. Just being close to him made her heart swell with joy, and her whole body was overwhelmed by the love that rippled through her. More than anything she wanted to love and cherish him and have him be part of her life from now on.

Yet that was not going to be possible, was it? He hadn't made any mention of loving her in return, and his kiss was simply a thank-you for being there when he'd needed her. And how could she even contemplate being with him when she could see how Alice had suffered and been set apart from her family simply because of her love for Robert Buchanan?

Ross eased himself away from her and she gave him a gentle smile and walked away, hurrying along the path as the snow began to fall.

The snow was still falling next day. Everything was covered in a thick white blanket, with drifts against the doors so that Izzy and Lorna had to dig out a path in order to reach their gate at the end of the front garden. A harsh wind caused the snowflakes to swirl all about them in a frenzy, and the branches of the trees swayed violently, swooping down towards the earth until the smaller branches cracked and split.

'This is really nasty,' Lorna said. 'I'm going to book my train ticket right now. There's no way

I'm going to be able to drive far in this, and I have to set out the day after tomorrow if I'm to reach my parents' house in time for Christmas Day.'

'Good idea,' Izzy murmured, putting away the shovel in the garden shed. 'How long will you be staying over there? Will you be spending New Year with them?'

Lorna shook her head. 'I have to be at work on New Year's Day,' she said. 'I'll have to come back on the thirty-first, but at least that will give me nearly a week with my family. I'll book a return ticket.'

Izzy hurried inside the house with Lorna, shaking the snow from her coat and hanging it up to dry in the cloakroom. She flicked the switch on the kettle to make a hot drink.

A few minutes later Lorna came into the kitchen. 'I thought you were making coffee?' she said.

'The electricity's off,' Izzy told her. 'I hope it's just a blip. Last time it went off the power lines were down, and it took at least twenty-four hours for the engineers to get it back on again.'

Lorna pulled a face. 'That's not great news, is

it? A lot of people around here use electricity for their heating, as well as for their cooking. It's going to be really hard for them to keep warm.'

By late afternoon it was becoming clear that the situation was not going to be remedied easily.

'The phone keeps ringing,' Lorna said. 'People wanting to check if we're in the same situation as them and worried about how long this is going to go on. There are some in the village who are really feeling the cold, and they haven't had a hot meal since yesterday. I think we ought to see if there's anything we can do to help.'

The doorbell rang, and Lorna hurried to answer it. Finn the postman was standing there. 'I'm coming around to tell everyone that Ross Buchanan has set up a soup kitchen at the castle. He has his own generator up there, and he's inviting people to go and get warm in the Great Hall.'

'That sounds like a wonderful gesture,' Lorna said.

'Aye. I've already taken up a lot of the old folk from the village. He asked me to come and let you girls know that you're very welcome. He's been ringing round most people, and a lot of them have taken him up on the offer.'

He made a rueful smile. 'Not your father, though, Izzy. You can imagine his answer, I expect. He says he'll make do with his charcoal barbecue for cooking food, and he has a coal fire in the living room to keep them warm. Mind you, he has offered to heat up soup and take it round to his neighbours. Your mother is busy taking tureens from house to house, checking that everyone is all right, bless her.'

'That's what I would have expected my mother to do,' Izzy said. 'As to my father, let's hope he doesn't burn the house down with his barbecue in the kitchen.'

'Is Ross going to have enough room if everybody in trouble turns up?' Lorna asked.

Finn nodded. 'His kitchen is huge, you know, and he says he's well stocked up with provisions. He's been out and about himself, fetching people or delivering heaters to those who want to stay in their own homes, but he asked me if I would come and check up on people in this area. Would you like me to take you up there now?'

'I think that would be a great idea,' Izzy said, glancing at Lorna for confirmation.

Lorna nodded. 'I'm cold through and through, and starving, so you don't need to ask me twice.'

'I know the neighbours round here are managing fairly well,' Izzy said, 'but one or two might like to come with us.'

They hunted around in the cupboards for food and drink that they could take with them to add to Ross's supplies. They chose anything that could be heated up and passed around. Izzy couldn't help thinking that it was just the sort of gesture she would have expected Ross to make. Why couldn't her father see that he was a good man?

Perhaps this would be a good time to ring him and put that question to him, while checking that her parents were coping well enough. She left Lorna with Finn, gathering more supplies, while she went to make the call.

'Well, maybe you're right,' her father said. 'I can't deny it's a good thing that he's doing. But it doesn't take away the fact that he's caused grief in more ways than one.'

'So you've been saying,' Izzy murmured. 'But you were wrong about the log cabin. It isn't meant for tourists at all, but as a special place for Alice and her family. He didn't tell you that, and maybe there are other things he hasn't thought fit to mention. Perhaps you're wrong in a lot of your assumptions? It seems to me that the two of you should get together and start talking to one another without arguing, if that's at all possible. You're both stubborn and proud, but it's high time that you listened properly to what each other has to say.'

'I don't need a slip of a girl to tell me what to do,' her father said in a blunt, abrasive tone. 'The Buchanans have goaded me endlessly over the years, and I don't need him to offer me charity, as if I'm some needy person who hasn't the wherewithal to take proper care of his family. I don't see why you keep associating with him the way you do. It goes against everything I've ever taught you.'

Izzy pulled in a steadying breath in an effort to calm herself. 'You know I love you and respect you, but I'm a grown woman and I have to make my own choices. I think you're wrong, in this instance, and I think you were wrong to cut Alice out of your life. She's our flesh and blood and she doesn't deserve any of this. She's lost her husband, and she's been very badly injured. The least you could do is go to see her and talk to her.'

She hesitated, afraid that she might have gone too far, but after a moment she plunged on. 'As for Ross, all I'm suggesting is that you take a small step to bridge the gap and allow you to start afresh. It wouldn't hurt you to take it. You wouldn't lose face by talking things through with him.' She paused once again, thinking things through. 'In fact, people might respect you more for having the courage to meet him halfway.'

'You don't know what you're asking of me. How can you not understand the way I feel—the way my father felt, and his father before him? Are *you* going to betray me, as well?'

His words shocked her, and frustrated her at the

same time. Izzy couldn't stop the faint tremor in her voice when she spoke to him again. 'I'm sorry you feel that way. You know how much I care for you and my mother. I love you both, and I don't want to be alienated from either of you. That's not what I want at all. I just want you to try to look at things from a different point of view.' She sighed heavily. 'I can see that's not going to be possible. I have to go.'

She cut the call and stood for a moment, thinking over what had been said. It was hopeless, trying to talk to her father about the Buchanans or about Alice. Her mother had been trying to change his views for years to no avail. He was like a brick wall—immovable, unyielding—and too proud for his own good.

In the Great Hall of the castle the banqueting table was laden with food, and people were helping themselves to steaming hot potatoes cooked in their jackets, with savoury fillings like cheese, curried sauces and baked beans, along with a selection of meat dishes, rice and soup.

'Has Maggie been doing all of this cooking?'

Izzy asked, as Ross ladled hot soup into a mug. He handed it to her and she wrapped her fingers around it to warm herself.

'No. Maggie prepared the meat dishes, but she had to go and see to her own family. Alice and I have done a lot of the work. It's amazing what she can do from a wheelchair, and she has been trying to stand every now and again to do things. I suppose it's good therapy. The children are loving every minute of it.'

'I think it's fantastic,' Lorna said, helping herself to coffee from a percolator. 'And there are so many people here. It's like a party. You've turned what might have been a miserable time into something marvellous.'

'I suppose I've been thinking of it as something like a welcome home party for Alice,' Ross said. 'Actually, it's really good to have everyone here. It's great to see everyone enjoying themselves. It's as though they've come together to support one another.'

'That's very true,' Izzy remarked, looking around. Alice was the centre of attention, and it was good to see her face lit up with happiness. She was well and truly back among the people of the village, and if her own family were not present in their entirety, at least she could take comfort in the fact that she was accepted by everyone else.

'Shall we escape to the library?' Ross murmured. 'It's great in here, but I've been surrounded by people for several hours and I wouldn't mind a bit of peace and quiet.'

She went with him, enjoying the sanctuary of the library, where bookshelves lined the walls and a magnificent old writing table faced the long window that overlooked the garden. There was a couch in there, with soft, luxurious upholstery, along with armchairs that faced the grand fireplace, where coals burned brightly and flames flickered orange and gold.

'I thought you might like to see the floor plans for the lodge,' he said. 'I showed them to Alice yesterday, and she was very pleased with the layout. We're still having furniture moved in there, so I haven't shown her the house itself as yet. I want her to see the finished product.' He removed a collection of papers from the desk drawer and came over to her. 'Come and sit with me?' he suggested, and Izzy went with him to the couch, sinking back against the brocade cushions.

He draped an arm around her, drawing her close. 'The main living-room window of the lodge looks out over the loch—see?' he said, showing her the papers. 'It gets the sun in the afternoon, pretty much as we do in the living room here.'

'I can see why she likes the layout,' Izzy commented, snuggling against the warmth of his chest. 'It all flows so smoothly, doesn't it? There's the living room, a huge dining-kitchen and a utility room downstairs, with the kitchen overlooking the garden…and upstairs there are *en suite* bathrooms and windows that look out over the mountains.' She smiled up at him. 'She must be longing to set foot in it.'

'I'm sure she is. It'll be a month or so before she's properly back on her feet, though, I imagine.'

Izzy was looking at some of the other papers in the bundle he had brought from the desk.

Some were plans for renovations to the castle itself, but one seemed to be more relevant to the land beyond the castle. 'What's this?' she asked. 'It looks like the river at the point of one of the falls.'

'It is. We often have flooding just below that point. I think it's due to debris being swept down from higher up, blocking the natural course of the river. I've had an expert take a look at it, and he's recommended that we dredge out part of the riverbed and build up the area where the debris collects. It should make the river flow much better, with fewer problems along the course.'

'Is this why my father has trouble with the salmon run?' she asked.

He nodded. 'Probably. The riverbed silts up in certain parts and causes problems further downstream. I think my father tried to put it right over the years, but nothing ever worked satisfactorily. When the dredging is finished that should all be sorted out, and Stuart shouldn't have any more problems.'

She put the papers to one side. 'I wish you

would explain all this to my father, if you ever get the chance. I don't know how to make him listen to me, and neither does my mother. All I know is that you don't deserve any of the flak that's been coming your way.' She reached up to him and cupped his face lightly in her hands. His slightly puzzled expression gave way to surprise and then pleasure when she drew him towards her and kissed him soundly on the mouth.

He didn't need any further bidding, and within a minute or two she was lying back against the cushions being thoroughly kissed in return. His hands moved over her, thrilling her with every gentle brush of his fingers, and his lips trailed over her face, her throat, dipping down to linger on the gentle swell of her breasts.

'Did I ever tell you how much I love having you around?' he asked. He swooped to claim her lips once more, stifling any answer she might have given. Then his fingers trailed over the length of her arm, tracing a path to her hand. He lifted her palm to his lips and kissed her tenderly, planting soft kisses over each finger in turn. 'I wish you would come and stay here over Christmas,' he said. 'You don't know how much that would mean to me—and to Alice and the children.'

'I wish I could,' she whispered, sadness sweeping through her. She returned his kisses, letting her hands glide over him, savouring the feel of his strong muscles and the length of his spine.

Then she laid her hands on his shoulders and gently eased him away from her, bringing herself up to a sitting position once more.

'Have I done something to upset you?' he asked.

She shook her head. 'No, nothing—nothing at all.' She looked at him. 'I wish I could stay. I wish I could be here at Christmas with you and Alice. But I can't. Perhaps I can slip away in the morning, just for an hour or so, but I have to be with the rest of my family—with my parents and grandparents. They're expecting me to be there. They want me to be there.'

His mouth made a rueful smile. 'What you mean, and what you're not saying, is that your father would blow his top if he knew that you were spending Christmas with me.'

'I'm working on him,' she said. 'I'm trying to get him to change the way he thinks.'

Ross stood up in one fluid movement. 'How long was it that Alice was married to my brother? He didn't change in all that time.'

Her gaze was troubled. 'I don't know how else to handle this,' she said.

'You don't have to.' Ross held out his hand to help her up from the couch. 'Loyalty is a finicky concept. I dare say there are always going to be losers.' He made a grimace. 'We should go back and join the others.'

When they went back into the Great Hall the assembled crowd was mellow, replete from all the good food and warm from the fire that burned in the magnificent fireplace. Villagers were chatting, one to the other, while Molly and Cameron were playing with other young-sters in between helping themselves to cookies from the table.

A local businessman came to take Ross to one side, and Izzy noticed that Lorna was across the other side of the room, talking to Greg and Finn.

Alice was in her wheelchair, but she saw Izzy standing by the door and came towards her.

'We're getting short on mulled wine,' Alice said. 'Do you want to come into the kitchen with me to make some more? I can manage most things, but I'm not so good at lifting things down from shelves.'

'Of course. Just tell me what you need and we'll make it together.'

No one had ventured into the kitchen, preferring to stay with the hub of activity in the Great Hall and the drawing room. Alice fetched a bottle of red wine from the rack and poured it into a pan on the hob, and then turned on the heat.

'I'll add some honey and sliced orange,' Alice said, going over to the fridge. 'We'll need some cinnamon sticks and ginger, too. They're on the shelf up there, if you could reach them down for me.'

Izzy obliged, adding them to the mix. 'That looks lovely,' she said. 'What a beautiful rich colour.'

Alice dipped a spoon into the liquid and tasted it. 'I think we need some cloves, and maybe a quarter cup of brandy. That should do it.'

Izzy looked around the kitchen for cloves while Alice added the brandy. 'We'll let that simmer for a few minutes,' Alice said. She glanced at Izzy. 'It's so good to be back here at last.' She was lost for a moment in a silent reverie. 'Robert was planning on coming back, you know.'

Izzy nodded. 'Ross said as much. I was a bit surprised at that, because I know Robert had some issues about being here. I wasn't sure how deep the rivalry went between them.'

Alice smiled. 'I know they were always fighting, but I think that was just the exuberance of youth…two young men growing up and battling for supremacy. It ended when they realised that they were equals. The one thing they had in common was their love of this place. They both had ideas about how it should be run, but their father would never let them do anything. He always thought he knew best.'

'Like my father,' Izzy said with a wry smile.

'Exactly like Pops.' A wistful expression flitted across Alice's face. 'I can't believe I used to call him that—it was such an endearing name. I thought the world of him. I still do.' She gazed up at Izzy. 'Only I fell in love with Robert. I knew all about the friction between the two families—how could I not?—but Robert and Ross were so kind to me after my parents died, and Robert... To me he was such a wonderful man—slightly flawed, but full of energy and re-belliousness. I couldn't help myself. I didn't want to hurt Pops, but I knew he would stop me from being with Robert and that's why I left.'

'Did you have any regrets...?' Izzy frowned. 'I mean, I know you must have, because I know you wouldn't have wanted to hurt my mother or my father, but what about Ross? Weren't you and he a couple at one time? Did you worry about what he would feel?'

Alice sent her an oblique glance. 'I know that's what everybody said, and I encouraged them to think that way. I thought maybe Pops would think it was the lesser of two evils if I was going around with Ross and not with Robert... But Ross was never in love with me. He pretended to be, to tease Robert, and he'd take me out and about on the estate, or buy me lunch in some out-of-the-way place so I could talk about my troubles, but we both knew that you were the only one he ever wanted.'

Izzy's brows shot up. 'That can't be true. Surely I would have known.' She was stunned by that revelation.

Alice shook her head. 'He used to try to talk to you whenever he met up with you by accident in the village, but you always kept the meetings short. He said you seemed to like him, but you would never look twice at him because your family was so set against the Buchanans, and he wouldn't push it because he knew you could be hurt. I think that's why he followed Robert and me to the Lake District. He knew after the furore that erupted that you would be even more determined to stay away from him. You wouldn't risk going against the family. So when Robert told him about a job that had come up at the hospital, he applied for it.'

Izzy stared at her. 'You've known this all this while? Yet you never said anything—you didn't even hint at it.'

'Ross asked me not to say anything.' Alice stirred the wine. 'I'm only talking about it now because I see the way you look at him, the way he looks at you, and I made that promise when the situation was different. You have to make the decision. Ross will never make it for you. All I can say is that I followed my heart, and though I don't regret what I did it *has* been hard to take the consequences of being cut off from the people I love. I went into it blindly, not knowing what might happen but hoping Pops would come round eventually. You, at least, will know what to expect.'

Izzy laid a hand on Alice's shoulder. 'Thank you for telling me all this. I'm sorry for the way you've had to suffer all these years, and I'm glad that Ross has brought you back here to us.'

Alice acknowledged that with a smile. 'We should pour the wine into a serving dish,' she said after a while. 'Or perhaps it would be better in one of those heat-resistant serving jugs.' She indicated a cupboard, and Izzy went to have a look.

'Okay, we'll take this back into the Great Hall, shall we?' Izzy suggested.

Her head was whirling with all that Alice had told her. Suddenly she had a completely different perspective on things. What was she to do? Could she follow her heart, let Ross know that she loved him and risk the wrath of her father, or should she put family above everything?

What was it that Ross had said about her father? *'How long was it that Alice was married to my brother? He didn't change in all that time.'*

CHAPTER TEN

'ARE you sure the roads are clear enough for you to drive over there? We're expecting more snow, and that wind's getting up again.' Izzy's mother was worried.

'I'll be fine. I'll drive carefully, I promise.' Izzy gave her a hug. 'I'll be back in time to help you with the Christmas dinner.'

She was gathering up Christmas presents from the kitchen table when her father came into the room. 'You're not actually going up there?' He was frowning heavily. 'It's Christmas morning. What on earth are you thinking of?'

'I'm thinking of Alice and the children,' Izzy said. 'I have some presents for them, and I want to wish them well.'

'But it's Buchanan's place. How can you be

going up *there*?' His scowl deepened as he looked at the parcels in her arms. 'I suppose you have a present for him as well, don't you?'

'I don't have a problem with Ross Buchanan,' Izzy said calmly. 'Just the opposite, in fact. Nor do I have a problem with Alice. I *want* to see them. I'll only be gone for an hour.'

'So you'd go against everything I believe in? All my principles?'

'That's just it. They're *your* principles, not mine. I'm sorry if that upsets you, but I think you're living in the past. It's time to move on and start a new way of life.'

'Why should I do that? Why should I abandon everything that I believe in?'

'Because it hurts the people that you love and the people who love you.' Izzy gazed at her father, trying to appeal to his better nature. 'It was your attitude that made Alice leave without saying anything. She didn't want to go against you, but you left her no choice. She ran away so that you wouldn't stop her. I'm not going to do that. I will always tell you what's in my mind and what I want to do. You might not always like it, but how you deal with it is up to you.'

He returned her gaze steadily, unflinching, but she thought she saw his shoulders relax a fraction, and that gave her a pause for thought. Was that what had been bothering him most of all? Had he thought she would simply walk out of his life in the same way Alice had done?

She said slowly, 'I think you should stop concentrating on the bad side of the Buchanans and think about all the good Ross has done. He is not his father or his grandfather. He has a set of principles that are every bit as strong as yours. Those are what make him the man he is—the man who goes out day in and day out to save the lives of people who are injured, the man who looks after his brother's wife and children. If nothing else, you should respect him for that.'

She left the house then and drove to Ross's home, the beautiful castle that had withstood the test of time on its craggy promontory overlooking the loch.

'Happy Christmas.' Ross greeted her with a

smile. 'I wasn't sure whether you would make it after all, but it is so good to see you. Did you have any problem coming here?'

Izzy shook her head. 'It's good to see you, too. How are things going with you and Alice and the children? Have you had a good morning so far?'

'We're having a great time.' He studied her briefly as he showed her into the Great Hall. 'I'm sure there's a lot you're not telling me, but we'll set that aside, shall we? Come and see everybody. They're still opening their presents in the drawing room.'

Izzy followed him, stopping to greet Alice and the children and hand out presents. They in turn gave her gifts that brought a smile to her face. 'An angora wool scarf and lovely perfume... exactly what I wanted.'

Alice exclaimed with delight over her gift of a cashmere sweater, and the children showed her their new toys and asked for help in undoing all the ties that held them in place in the boxes.

Izzy gave Ross a brightly wrapped parcel, and

he looked startled. 'You bought me a present? I wasn't expecting that at all.'

She smiled. 'I wasn't sure what would be the best thing to get for you,' she murmured. 'But then I hit on an idea and this seemed like just the thing. I hope you like it.'

He carefully opened his present, gazing down at it in wonder. It was a bottle of wine, but the glass was specially tinted and etched with a picture of the castle against a background of mountains, and the whole was highlighted with touches of gold, to make it look as though the sun was shining down over everything.

'It's actually your own wine that's in the bottle,' she said. 'I had to do a bit of conniving with Maggie and the man who does the bottling to make it just right.'

He was still staring at the bottle. He placed it down on the top of a cupboard, putting it out of harm's reach and in pride of place at the centre. 'That is such a great gift,' he said. 'Thank you for that.' His smile warmed her through and through. 'I wonder if we could reproduce them and make special presentation bottles for the winery.' He wound his arms around her and kissed her full on the mouth, uncaring that Alice and the children were watching their every move.

He broke off the kiss after a minute or two and turned to face the others. Molly and Cameron, after looking at them wide-eyed for a second, lost interest and went on examining their toys. Alice had a wide grin on her face.

'I'm going to take Izzy to the library,' he said. 'I have a present waiting for her in there.'

'We'll be fine,' Alice said. 'You go ahead. Just remember I've planned dinner for a couple of hours' time.'

'I have to be back home way before then.' Izzy laughed.

Ross had taken hold of her hand, though, and was leading her towards the library at a brisk pace.

'I have two presents for you,' he said. 'The first is something that I thought you would enjoy… something to make you feel cosseted at the end of a hard day. Lorna said you didn't have one— not quite like this, anyway.'

He had bought her a silk robe, beautifully hand-embroidered and exquisite in its entirety. She gasped. 'It's lovely,' she murmured. 'I wasn't expecting anything—especially not this.'

'Hmm…I have to admit I've had a few problems over this robe—I kept thinking of how you would look when you were wearing it. I just can't keep up with the cold showers.'

Her cheeks flushed hotly pink, but he had already turned away, and now drew out a small box from the bureau. 'This is the present that I really wanted to give you,' he said softly. 'The trouble is, I'm not at all sure that you will accept it.'

The breath seemed to have left her body all at once. He opened up the box and inside, nestling on a velvet cushion, was the most perfect diamond ring she had ever seen.

Tears sprang to her eyes. 'Is that what I think it is?' she asked, her voice husky.

He nodded. 'It's an engagement ring. I think you must know that I love you—that I have always loved you, Izzy. What I want more than anything is for you to say that you will be my wife. Will you marry me?'

Tears began to trickle down her face. 'I want to say yes,' she whispered. 'I really want to say yes. Because I love you, too. I've known it for some time. But I don't think we can ever be happy if my father is alienated from us. There would always be that anguish at the back of my mind. I want to be with you, Ross, but I can't.'

'Are you sure about that? We could ask him to give us his blessing, but if he won't we could marry anyway. At least you would have tried to win him round.'

She shook her head. 'I want to marry in the church in the village, with my family all around me and my father walking me down the aisle. I don't want to have to hide or to flinch or to beg forgiveness for my actions. I want my family to be happy for me. I just don't see how that is ever going to happen.'

He drew in a deep breath and closed up the box. He put it away once more in a drawer in the bureau, and then closed up the door. 'It will stay there,' he said, 'until the day you change your mind.'

Izzy's emotions threatened to overwhelm her. Had she really just turned down the man she loved? It was unbearable even to think about it.

She started the drive home just a short time later. If Alice guessed that something was wrong she said nothing, and Ross put on a bluff exterior as though all was right with the world. It was only his eyes that gave him away. There was a bleakness there when he thought no one was looking, and it cut Izzy to the quick.

Christmas dinner with her family was generally a happy time. Today her grandparents were there to share the meal with them, along with uncles and aunts and cousins, and then the neighbours, who came round to share a drink afterwards and watch the Queen's speech on the television.

If her father was more quiet than usual no one except Izzy and her mother seemed to notice, and the neighbours forgot themselves enough to mention that Ross had invited everyone over for the Hogmanay celebrations in less than a week's time.

'It was on the day when the power lines were down,' one of the neighbours said. 'He said we were all invited. He's planning on making it a tradition to hold a party up at the castle. I think it should be good. It was generous of him to have us all over there when we were cold and hungry, don't you think?'

Izzy's mother glanced at her husband. 'I thought it was a nice thing to do. He sent us an invitation for the party through the post. We weren't there that day, you see.'

'Ah…yes, that's true.' The neighbour looked uncomfortable for a moment, and then sought for a way to change the subject. 'I thought the Queen's speech was very good this year, didn't you? She was showing us how people triumph over the bad times, and how people can be uplifted even when they have been suffering.'

They all started to talk about the TV schedules and disaster was averted—for the time being at any rate. Izzy helped to clear away the crockery from the dinner table, and lost herself in thoughts of what might have been if only circumstances had been different. Her body might well be here, in her parents' kitchen, but her soul was away across the miles by the loch, with the Laird of Glenmuir.

She didn't see Ross again in the week that followed, though she heard about a helicopter rescue when he airlifted an injured man to hospital following an accident on the main road to Inverness. His patient had suffered cardiac contusions, and by all accounts it had been touch and go for a while, but Ross had managed to get him there safely, and according to the newspaper reports he was now recovering from his ordeal.

The weather became more and more treacherous as New Year's Eve dawned, with the wind rising and blowing the snowflakes this way and that, so that Izzy had to keep her head down to avoid it blowing into her eyes whenever she went to put out seeds and raisins on the bird table in her parents' garden.

'They say there are trees coming down in the highest areas,' her mother said. 'According to the news report they're worried about hazards on the roads and on the railways. There was something on the television just a little while ago about a branch coming down on the line that passes by the village. I didn't hear that they've put a halt to any of the trains, though. Isn't Lorna supposed to be coming back today?'

Izzy was suddenly on alert. 'Did they say the branch had actually come down on the line? Surely they must have stopped the trains if that's the case?'

'I didn't hear all of it,' her mother said. 'Steven from next door came to ask if your father could give him a hand with the logs for his fire. He was having trouble stacking them in the shed.'

Izzy turned on the television set and tuned to a news programme. 'There's nothing,' she said in frustration. 'Lorna *was* supposed to be coming back around about this time. She has to work tomorrow, and there's only the one train running because of the holidays. I think I'll try and reach her on her mobile to see what's happening. I need to know that she's safe.'

There was no answer from Lorna's mobile, and Izzy paced the room in frustration. Maybe she had switched it off, or perhaps she was in a poor signal area. Either way, Izzy was left feeling helpless. She sent a text message, asking Lorna to get in touch.

A few minutes later her phone rang, and she seized it eagerly. It wasn't Lorna, though. It was the ambulance service, calling her out to attend to what they were calling a 'major event'.

'We need you here as soon as you can manage it,' the controller said. 'If you can get hold of Ross, we need him, too. He's not answering his phone, so it may be that he's in an area where he can't get a good signal.'

Izzy rang the landline at the castle and Maggie answered. 'He's busy with the preparations for this evening's Hogmanay celebrations,' she said. 'He's been out and about all morning fetching supplies, and then he's been sorting things out in the cellar and what have you. I'll see if I can find him.'

Izzy hurried to get into her emergency medic uniform. 'Where are you off to?' her mother asked.

'The railway line by the embankment,' Izzy said. 'You were right about the branch coming down—except that it was more than a branch, and it came down just as the train was approaching. The driver pulled on the brakes, but he didn't quite make it in time and the first carriage of the train has derailed. We need all the help we can get. We don't know how many people were on the train. I don't even know if Lorna is one of the people who are injured.'

Her father started to put on his coat. 'I'll come with you,' he said. 'They may need help with lifting. I expect Steven from next door will come along, too.'

Her mother did some rapid thinking. 'I'll organise some vacuum flasks, for soup and the like. You go on ahead. I'll get someone to drive me there.'

Izzy drove as fast as she dared, given the road conditions. Steven and her father followed on behind in Steven's car. Izzy didn't know what to expect, but any derailment was likely to be very bad news.

Ross was there ahead of her, tending to the wounded who were being brought out on stretchers. 'So far we're dealing mainly with broken limbs and cuts from twisted metal. There's been nothing too serious up to now.'

'Lorna was supposed to be on this train,' she said. 'Has there been any news of her? I keep trying her phone, but there's no answer.'

He shook his head. 'Nothing so far. All the people who were in the carriages behind the first one have managed to get out, and they've been taken to the community hall. Lorna wasn't among them.'

He waved a hand towards the carriage. 'We've brought out everybody we could reach, but there's still a part of the carriage that we can't enter. The metal has buckled, making it difficult for anyone to get in there. And we can't go in through the windows because they are too distorted.'

'What about the fire crew?' Alice looked around. She couldn't see any heavy lifting equipment in place.

'They've brought in as many people as they can, but with the holidays they're short-handed. Some people have gone away for the New Year.

The lifting equipment is on its way, but it will take some time to get it into position.' He looked concerned. 'The trouble is, I *know* that there are people trapped inside, and I'm worried in case they need urgent help. There's a lot of glass about, and if they have been cut they could be bleeding badly.'

And Lorna could be one of them. 'Is there anything we can do to get through to them? I'm quite slender, so perhaps I could squeeze into a small gap?'

'Maybe if we have a word with the fire crew and gather together some helpers we could sort something out.'

In the end it was decided that there was a small section where it might be possible for Izzy to squeeze through into the compartment. The men worked together to open up the section, using what equipment they had to widen the space. Inside the cavity they could hear somebody groaning in pain. After a while the sound stopped, and Izzy began to worry.

'I'm going in now,' she said. Her father, Ross

and Steven steadied the metalwork while she struggled into the cabin. She shone a torch around. In the far corner a woman lay crumpled between the seats. It wasn't Lorna, and she couldn't see anyone else in there. There was a lot of blood, and as Izzy investigated she could see that it was coming from a large gash on the woman's arm.

'I'm going to apply a pressure pad to try to stem the bleeding,' she called back to Ross. 'And I'll put in an intravenous line.' She worked quickly, giving the woman oxygen and trying to resuscitate her. Finally the woman's eyes flickered, and Izzy breathed a faint sigh of relief. 'We'll get you to hospital as soon as we can,' she said.

Shining the torch around, she tried to discover if there was anyone else inside the carriage. 'There was a man,' the woman said. 'I think he's trapped under the seat.'

Izzy went to investigate where the woman had indicated. Her pulse quickened and her mouth went dry as she saw a hand sticking out from under the metalwork. 'I need some help in here,' she said. 'There's a man beneath the seat. I can feel a pulse, very faint, but he's definitely still alive.'

It was some five minutes before they could open up the gap wide enough for Ross to crawl through. 'Your father has his back against the metalwork, holding it up,' he told her. 'Steven is helping, and the fire crew have gone to get more cutting equipment. In the meantime, let's see if we can lever this seat off the injured man.'

He looked around and found a loose bar of metal lying around—possibly one of the handrails, or maybe a piece from the table. 'See if you can heave the seat upwards while I try to lever it out of the way.'

Between them they pushed and pulled, until they felt the metalwork start to give way. 'I think it's coming,' Ross said. 'Okay, get your breath and then let's try again.'

Finally the seat tipped backwards, freeing the man enough for them to carefully pull him away to safety. But then there was a grinding noise and a piece of the overhead luggage rack started to fall away. Ross moved quickly to cover Izzy with his body and at the same time protect their patient. The piece of rack slithered away and fell to the floor with a clatter.

'Are you all right in there?' Izzy's father queried sharply.

'We're fine,' Izzy called back as Ross's arms closed around her. 'At least I think we are. I'm not so sure about Ross.' She looked at him. 'Are you hurt?'

'We're all okay,' Ross said. 'Let's get to our patient.' He knelt down beside the man.

'I'm going to put a tube in his throat to help him breathe,' Ross told Izzy. 'He'll need fluids, and splints for his arm and leg. I can see there's definitely a fracture to the tibia, and it looks as though the arm could be broken, too.'

Both of the injured people were given painkillers. When Izzy assessed their vital signs she found that the woman's condition was stabilising, but the man's blood pressure was low and he was in a critical condition. At least he was still alive.

The fire crew opened up the gap so that the paramedics could go in with stretchers, and soon

Izzy emerged from the carriage into the light of day once more. Her father looked bone weary from his exertions to keep open the escape route, as did his neighbour.

'Thank you both for your help,' Ross said, as he came out into the open air and straightened up. 'We couldn't have done it without you.'

'You didn't do a bad job yourself,' her father said. 'You and my daughter both. I was worried for her safety, as well as for the people in there, but I knew you would look after her.'

Ross's mouth curved. 'I would always look out for your daughter's safety,' he answered. 'I love her, and I want her to be my wife. She's the only one who appears to have any doubts.'

Izzy's father appeared to be shocked by that revelation. He looked from one to the other but made no comment, and Izzy guessed that he was trying to absorb what Ross had said. 'I must go and see to our patients,' she said.

'Me, too,' Ross commented, starting to follow her. He paused, turning to look back. 'I'm not sure that I feel too much like celebrating,' he murmured, 'but I don't want to let anybody down, and the Hogmanay festivities will go on as planned. It would be good to see you and your wife there with us.'

They went over to the ambulances and supervised the transfer of the injured people to the vehicles. 'I expect the man will go straight up to Theatre after he's been properly assessed,' Izzy said. 'I still can't think what's happened to Lorna, but she definitely wasn't on the train.'

'Maybe she decided to come back by road?' Ross said. He glanced at Izzy. 'Will I see *you* tonight up at the castle?'

'Oh, yes,' she murmured. 'Like you, I don't feel much like celebrating after all that's gone on today, but I do want to see an end to this year. I'm hoping that the New Year will bring fresh hope for all of us.'

CHAPTER ELEVEN

'Wow!' Ross stared at Izzy as though he was seeing her for the first time. 'You look beautiful. I'm almost lost for words.'

'That would be a very strange thing,' Izzy said. Inside, though, she was glowing at the compliment. She had chosen the dress especially for this evening. It was made of a soft, floaty material that swirled around her calves as she walked. The shoulder straps were thin, lightly spangled strips, and the bodice fitted her to perfection. Her shoes sparkled, too, complementing the straps and the tiny clips that she wore in her hair.

'Welcome to the *ceilidh*,' he said, taking her hand and drawing her towards the Great Hall. 'There's dancing in the main reception room, and music in here, too. We thought we'd have the bagpipes later on, nearer to midnight and the welcoming in of the New Year.'

Izzy looked around at the gathering of people. They were all chatting and laughing, and generally making merry. She knew all of them, either from the village or from her work at the A&E unit, and she acknowledged those who looked her way.

Then she stared along the length of the banqueting table. 'I thought we saw a feast that day when the film crew were here, and again when you set out the food for the people who'd lost their electricity, but this—this is something else again. You've done us proud.'

'Molly and Cameron like it, anyway. Cameron's eyes were like saucers. He helped us to set it all out, but I think he had a few nibbles along the way, so his tummy's quite full at the moment.'

'You must have been so busy doing all this,' she said. 'Or did you get caterers in?'

'It was a combined effort, really, between me and Alice, the children and Maggie. Mary from the shop came along and brought some food to add to the selection, and Greg brought some wine and some friends. Alice's sister and her husband have come over from the Lake District with their children to join in the celebrations and stay with us for a few days, so Alice is very happy.' He glanced around at the assembled crowd. 'Lorna's here, too. Apparently she came home by car as far as the A&E unit, and Greg brought her in from there.'

'That's a relief. Though I rang her parents to find out if they knew anything, and they told me she'd set off with a friend rather than come back by train.' She glanced at him. 'Have you heard anything more about the casualties from this afternoon? I rang the hospital earlier, and they said the man was undergoing surgery for chest injuries. Everyone else was doing reasonably well.'

'Yes, I asked one of the senior house officers to ring me and let me know what was happening. He said that the man had come through the operation all right, and that his vital signs were improving. I guess his New Year gift is that he's alive to see it.'

She tilted her head to listen to the music that

sounded all around. 'I'm not sure where that's coming from,' she said, 'but it's beautiful—lovely Highland music.'

'Ah, that's from my hidden music system. It's meant to fill your soul with dreams of romance.' He draped an arm around her and immediately her senses tipped into chaotic activity. Warmth from his fingers spread along her waist and over her hip, pooling in her abdomen. She looked up at him. She loved this man. Why could she not tell him what he wanted to hear? That she was happy to be with him at whatever the cost?

'I take it that your father hasn't said anything about coming along this evening?' he murmured.

She shook her head. 'I haven't seen him since we left the railway line this afternoon.'

'Never mind. Let's try to enjoy ourselves anyway. Shall we go through to the reception room? It's more lively in there. We have people who can play the piano and the guitar, and there are even some who can sing. We might even have a dance together. Perhaps I can persuade you that it wouldn't be so bad to be married to me? I could make you forget everything else so that there was only you and me.'

He held her close, looking down at her, and she wanted to say there and then, *That's all I want. Let's do it. Let's forget the outside world and think only of ourselves.*

In the reception room space had been cleared for dancing, and couples moved to the rhythm of the music, all of them having a good time. Across the room Izzy saw that Alice was sitting in her wheelchair and the children were by her side. Izzy and Ross made their way towards her, and a moment later Molly and Cameron went to join their cousins and other youngsters who had come to enjoy the festivities.

The musicians struck up a slow waltz, and Greg walked over to Alice. 'I'm your Prince Charming,' he said. 'Would you like to dance?'

Alice laughed softly. 'Well, now, I'd like to very much. But I think I might have a little bit of a problem there.'

'I can deal with problems,' he said. 'I have this magic touch, you see.' He held out his hands to her, though he was still some small distance away.

Alice carefully stood up. She straightened, took a moment to get her balance, and then she took a faltering step towards him, then another, and then another. He clasped her hands and drew her to him, and together they swayed to the music. All the people nearby watched and clapped, and a great cheer went around the room.

Ross held out his hands to Izzy. 'Shall we dance?' he asked softly. 'I'm definitely not Prince Charming, but I could do a fair representation of a lovesick Scottish laird.'

She went into his arms and danced with him. It was as though she was floating on air. He was everything she needed and wanted, and she made up her mind that for the next hour or so at least she would treasure this time with him and fill her heart with hope that one day her path would be smooth.

It was some time after eleven, when they had eaten all that they wanted for the moment and Izzy had sipped a glass or two of wine, chatting with friends and dancing with Ross, that there was a faint stirring at the other end of the room. Voices became hushed, and people turned to see that Izzy's parents had walked into the room.

'We meant to get here earlier,' her mother said, a little flustered. 'But the car wouldn't start. And there wasn't a taxi—well, there wouldn't be, would there, when Jock's at the party?'

There was a faint ripple of laughter throughout the room. 'You should have rung me,' Izzy said. 'You know I would have come and fetched you.'

Her father looked at her. 'And you full of the drink? I think not. I told your mother I would fix the car, and I did—didn't I?' He looked at her mother, his brows raised in a questioning manner.

Her mother became even more flustered. She looked around the room and said, 'Go on with your dancing, everyone. You're here to have a good time, not to look at us.'

Ross came to stand beside them. 'It's good to see you both here,' he said. 'I wasn't sure whether you would manage it.'

'Well, I've had time to do a lot of thinking,' her father said. 'I had to respect what you did this afternoon—looking after the people in the train and protecting Izzy when she might have been injured.' He frowned. 'And then I heard that you'd brought in dredging equipment to sort out the riverbed. That should certainly make a difference to my salmon fishing interests. I realise that I might have misjudged you. Maybe you're not so bad as I've been painting you.'

Ross laughed. 'I'm glad to hear it. Maybe you're not such a grouch as you make out. Anyway, I'm glad to see you here.' He glanced around. 'In fact, I was just going to tell everyone about the lighting of the torches. It was young Molly and Cameron who suggested to me that we ought to revive the tradition.'

He addressed the gathering of people. 'For anyone who wants to join in, we're going to have a procession around the castle walls. The lighting of the flame is done so that we dispense with the darkness of the past and take the knowledge and the wisdom from the old year into the new one. We forget the bad things that have happened in the previous year and carry the flame of hope and enlightenment into the New Year.'

He looked at Izzy's father. 'What do you say to that, Stuart?'

Her father nodded. 'I think Molly and Cameron have come up with a great idea. Like Izzy said to me a while ago, we should concentrate on the good in people. I've been very much taken up with the bad things that have happened in the past, and it took Molly and Cameron to show me that what makes for happiness in this world is the love of family.'

He looked across the room to where Alice was sitting beside Greg. He started towards her. 'I am sorry for all the hurt that I've caused you,' he said. 'I know that you did what you did for love, and I respect you for that. Can you forgive me?'

Alice lifted her arms to him and he bent towards her, holding her tight and whispering softly against her hair. After a while he released her, and she smiled up at him. 'Will you carry a torch for *me*, Pops?' she asked. 'I'm not really up to doing that for myself this year, but I promise you next year I shall join the procession.' Greg reached over and placed his hand on hers, emphasising that vow and silently offering support.

'I will, Alice,' Stuart said. 'I'll hold it high for the world to see.'

He turned back to face Ross, and Ross gave a wide smile and said, 'Come on, then, everyone. We have the torches ready in the kitchen, and we have to do the full circuit before midnight strikes. We want to be back here together to see this New Year in properly, don't we?'

Within minutes the procession of cheerful revellers took off around the walls of the castle, accompanied by the haunting sound of bagpipes, and Izzy looked up to see that the men stood at the top of the square tower, piping the torch bearers on their way.

The torches were set finally in a brazier on the flat roof of the tower, and fireworks were let off to shoot high into the sky. 'I think we should go inside,' Ross said after a while. 'It will soon be midnight, and we need to toast the New Year.'

The heavy chimes of the clock sounded the

midnight hour in the Great Hall and everyone joined in, counting down until the last chime rang out, and then a great cheer went up. Ross drew Izzy into his arms, kissing her with a thoroughness that took her breath away. All around her people were clinking glasses, toasting the New Year with champagne, but the champagne was on Izzy's lips, placed there by the man of her dreams.

Ross kept his arm around her as he led her towards the great fireplace. 'I want to make a speech,' he said, addressing the gathering once more. 'And you needn't groan, because it's a short one. There are only three points I want to make.'

Still sipping their champagne, everyone looked towards him. Izzy's parents were just a short distance away, toasting one another, and Alice and Greg and the children were close by, with Alice's sister next to her. Lorna stood with them, and behind her all the rest of the villagers, Izzy's friends and work colleagues, stood around.

'First, I thought this might be the right time to let you know that if there is anyone among you who wants to buy out their tenancy, and become owner of their land and property, I will be glad to have my lawyers draw up the appropriate papers. I'm sure we can agree fair terms.'

A hum of conversation started up.

'Just let me know over the next week or so if you're interested,' Ross said. 'And that brings me to my second statement. I know that some of our young people have been leaving the Highlands to go and live and work in the main towns and cities. I have plans for this estate, and plans to develop a winery—and I know you'll all be happy to go along with that, because you've been partaking of the wines all evening and coming back for more...'

There was laughter from the assembly.

'And I also want to go ahead with a timber plantation. For both of these projects I will need workers to keep them going. I'm looking for an estate manager, as well.' He paused for a moment, looking around. 'That's not all. I know you heard about the film crew that came here a while back. That was just the beginning, and I know that they are looking for extras to take part in the next production that will be done here. I'm sure we have some budding actors among our crowd.'

There was more laughter, and still they looked at him expectantly. 'You said there was a third thing,' Izzy's father said.

Ross looked at Izzy, and there was a question in his eyes. 'It concerns you and me,' he said softly, so that the others could not hear. 'Shall I be able to place that diamond ring on your finger, do you think?"

'Yes,' she said, smiling at him. 'You will.'

He faced the crowd once more. 'I'm hoping that we will see all of you at another gathering very shortly—in the church. That's if Izzy gives me the answer I want.'

He turned to look at her, reaching for her hand. 'Will you marry me, Izzy? Will you be my wife?'

Happiness glowed in her smile. 'I will, Ross.'

He kissed here there and then, sealing the bargain, and then turned to face the crowd once more. 'You're all welcome at the ceremony, and at the reception afterwards. We'll look forward to seeing you there.'

A cheer went up, loud enough to reach the rafters, but Izzy was barely aware of it because Ross was kissing her again, and that was all that mattered to her right then.

Some time later, when he finally released her, she gazed around to find that people were smiling and drinking and chatting to one another.

'We'll have to design a new coat of arms,' Ross said, glancing behind him at the shield above the fireplace. 'Buchanan and McKinnon.'

'Don't you mean McKinnon and Buchanan?' Izzy's father said pointedly.

Ross raised a dark brow. 'Are you trying to start an argument with me, Stuart?' he said.

'Argument? What makes you think that?' Her father's voice was sharp edged.

'Shall we say a touch of belligerence in your tone?'

'Oh, I see. So you're saying that I'm aggressive, are you? Me? I don't have an aggressive bone in my body.' Stuart McKinnon turned to scowl at the crowd. 'And I'll fight any man here who says different.' A wide grin spread over his face.

Laughter rang out. 'Way to go, Stuart.' Greg was chuckling.

'Aye.' Izzy's father raised a glass to her and Ross. Her mother joined him, lifting her own champagne flute. 'You have our blessing, both of you,' he said. 'May all your troubles be little ones.'

Ross squeezed Izzy, holding her close as she looked up at him. 'I think I'm the happiest girl in the world,' she told him.

There was a loud rapping on the outer door, and she frowned. 'Who could that be?'

'That will be someone I'm expecting,' Ross said. 'I believe it's our first-footer, come to see in the New Year with us.'

They went together to open the door, and there stood Jason Trent, the actor, tall and dark-haired, bearing gifts.

'I've brought coal,' Jason said, 'so that your hearth will always be warm, bread so that you will not go hungry, and a silver coin so that you may be prosperous into the New Year.'

'Come in,' Ross said. 'In return we'll give you whisky and good cheer, and food to fill you up.'

'Exactly what I wanted,' Jason said. 'And Lorna, of course. I take it she's here?'

'She is. She's waiting for you in the Great Hall. You know the way, don't you?'

Jason nodded, and grinned. He knew better than to expect Ross and Izzy to follow him. They were far too busy kissing.

MEDICAL™

Large Print

Titles for the next six months…

MILLS & BOON®

MEDICAL™

Large Print

November

THE SURGEON'S MIRACLE	Caroline Anderson
DR DI ANGELO'S BABY BOMBSHELL	Janice Lynn
NEWBORN NEEDS A DAD	Dianne Drake
HIS MOTHERLESS LITTLE TWINS	Dianne Drake
WEDDING BELLS FOR THE VILLAGE NURSE	Abigail Gordon
HER LONG-LOST HUSBAND	Josie Metcalfe

December

THE MIDWIFE AND THE MILLIONAIRE	Fiona McArthur
FROM SINGLE MUM TO LADY	Judy Campbell
KNIGHT ON THE CHILDREN'S WARD	Carol Marinelli
CHILDREN'S DOCTOR, SHY NURSE	Molly Evans
HAWAIIAN SUNSET, DREAM PROPOSAL	Joanna Neil
RESCUED: MOTHER AND BABY	Anne Fraser

January

DARE SHE DATE THE DREAMY DOC?	Sarah Morgan
DR DROP-DEAD GORGEOUS	Emily Forbes
HER BROODING ITALIAN SURGEON	Fiona Lowe
A FATHER FOR BABY ROSE	Margaret Barker
NEUROSURGEON...AND MUM!	Kate Hardy
WEDDING IN DARLING DOWNS	Leah Martyn

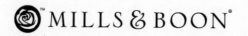

MILLS & BOON®